"You packing?"

"Packing what?" Clay asked.

"Condoms." Jo Beth slid her hand from his waist to the back pocket of his trousers and squeezed. "I'll bet you've got a couple in your wallet, right?"

"Yeah." He didn't blush. "So?" he said, with all the wariness of a man who had reached out to pet a house cat and found himself stroking a tiger instead.

"So I'm going to dance two more dances after this one, and then I'm going to the corral by the barn. There's a tack room in the northeast corner." She leaned into him, lightly touching her breasts to his chest. "It has a door. And a lock."

The bolt of lust that shot through Clay burned away all thoughts of propriety and what was or was not appropriate behavior at a wedding.

"I'll wait ten minutes," she said. "If you don't show up by then, I'll lock the door and play by myself."

Dear Reader,

I received more fan mail after the publication of *Good Time Girl* than for any other book I've written. Readers told me how much they liked the hot sex scenes and then asked when I was going to write Clay's story.

As an author, I had created Clay Madison strictly as a plot device to move the story along. He was a secondary character whose role was to make the hero of *Good Time Girl* jealous. Once he'd done that, I never expected to write about him again. Little did I know! Readers *loved* him. "What happens to Clay?" they asked. "Give us Clay's story!" they demanded.

It took me a while to figure out where life and love would eventually lead the sexy young bull rider. It took me a little while longer to find the woman who was strong and sexy enough to appeal to the rodeo champion he was destined to become. Much to my surprise (again!) another secondary character from *Good Time Girl* turned out to be exactly the right woman.

Happy reading,

Candace Schuler

Books by Candace Schuler

HARLEQUIN BLAZE
7—UNINHIBITED
27—GOOD TIME GIRL

HARLEQUIN TEMPTATION
557—PASSION AND SCANDAL
608—LUCK OF THE DRAW
648—OUT OF CONTROL

THE COWBOY WAY

Candace Schuler

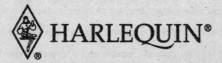

TORONTO • NEW YORK • LONDON
AMSTERDAM • PARIS • SYDNEY • HAMBURG
STOCKHOLM • ATHENS • TOKYO • MILAN • MADRID
PRAGUE • WARSAW • BUDAPEST • AUCKLAND

To all the romance readers who demanded Clay's story.

ISBN 0-373-79181-X

THE COWBOY WAY

1

"AH, TO HELL with it!" Jo Beth Jensen pushed back from her desk with enough force to send her chair crashing into the metal file cabinet behind her and shot to her feet. Yanking the straw cowboy hat off the peg by the door as she passed, she jammed it on her head and, spurs jangling discordantly with every step, stomped out of her office. "I'm going riding," she said to the round-faced Mexican woman who came out of the kitchen to see what all the commotion was about.

Esperanza Diego nodded complacently and disappeared back into the kitchen without saying a word. None of the cowhands Jo Beth passed on her way to the barn said a word to her, either. Anybody with one good eye and half a brain could tell at a glance that the jefe of the Diamond J was in the mood to kick some butt.

It was a mood she'd been in for some time now, off and on. Not that anyone blamed her. What with the three best hands on the place lost to the summer rodeo circuit, and turning the main house into fancy la-di-da accommodations for city slickers, and the wedding and all…it was enough to make anyone a mite cranky.

Added to which, they all knew she'd spent the morning holed up inside the stuffy little office across from the kitchen, wrestling with columns of numbers that most likely added up to just barely enough. So they all certainly understood, even sympathized with, her obvious desire to stomp the shit out of someone—just so long as that unlucky someone was someone else. As a result of this very natural desire to spare their individual derrieres, the barn was empty of human habitation when she reached it.

"José!" she hollered, pausing just inside the door to give her eyes a moment to adjust to the shadowed interior. "T-Bone! Damn it, where the hell is everybody?"

A lone horse nickered in answer.

"Cowboys." Jo Beth shook her head. "Bunch of no 'count, lily-livered good-for-nothings. Always running off at the slightest sign of trouble. Irresponsible sons o'…" Her voice trailed off as she neared the occupied stall. "Hey there, Bella," she crooned, reaching into her breast pocket to fish out one of the peppermint candies she always carried for her pampered favorite. "How're you doing, sweetheart?"

The horse nickered again and thrust its head over the stall door, neck stretched out in greeting. Jo Beth offered her hand, palm up. The mare lipped the small red-and-white pinwheel delicately, accepting it as her due, then dropped her head and butted it against Jo Beth's chest. Jo Beth touched her forehead to the mare's, and felt her bad mood start to dissolve.

Bella was her best and dearest friend, a sweet-tempered strawberry roan with a freckled white stripe on her nose and three white stockings. She'd been a champion barrel racer in her prime, and was still a damned fine cutting horse as long as you didn't work her too hard or too long. She was patient, polite, and undemanding, without an ounce of foolishness or folly in her. A woman couldn't ask for a steadier or more dependable companion.

"What say you and me go for a ride?" Jo Beth whispered into the mare's velvety ear. "Get ourselves a little fresh air and exercise. Stretch our legs. Work some of the kinks out. Hmm?" She lifted a lead shank from the hook between the stalls as she spoke, clipped it onto the mare's halter, and led her out of the barn and into the scorching Texas sunshine.

Fifteen minutes later she gathered up the reins and swung into the saddle. Bella took a little dancing sideways step, the powerful muscles of her shoulders and flanks twitching as she sensed her rider's restlessness and impatience.

"Tell Esperanza not to wait dinner on me," Jo Beth said to the lone cowhand who'd decided it was safe to show his face now that she was mounted up.

She held Bella to a walk as they exited the stable yard, eased her to a slow, rolling canter when they'd cleared the little hillock and the stand of scrub pine and oak trees behind the barn, and then let her have her head when the land flattened out. They raced hell-bent-for-leather for a few exhilarating moments, the hot wind whistling past their ears, Bella's red mane and tail streaming, her hooves pounding against the hard-packed earth.

Jo Beth bent low over the mare's neck, her thick braid whipping out behind her, and the coil of catch rope looped over the saddle horn bouncing against her thigh. She wished they could run forever. But Bella was blowing hot and breathing hard, her thick barrel bellowing in and out between Jo Beth's legs. Jo Beth reined in, bringing the pulse-pounding, ground-pounding gallop back down to canter, and then to a trot, and, finally, to a walk. Bella shook her head, jingling her bridle as if in protest at the slowdown, but she settled into it, more than content with the leisurely pace.

Jo Beth sighed and tried to be content, too, but she was still restless. Still edgy. Still agitated and dissatisfied and riled up. And it wasn't *all* because of the three hands who'd quit on her to follow the summer rodeo circuit, leaving her shorthanded when she needed them most, or the half dozen city slickers who were due to invade the Diamond J in less than a week, or her best friend's wedding at which she had agreed to be—God help her—the maid of honor. It wasn't even the bookkeeping.

It was that damned Clay Madison!

If she'd been getting laid regular, it wouldn't be so bad. But it had been over six months since that weekend in Dallas with Jim, the cattle broker, and she'd gone without for four months before that. It'd been so long, she'd almost forgotten what it was she was missing. And then Clay Madison had swaggered onto the scene with that lazy, loose-hipped, loose-kneed cowboy saunter of his and had reminded her of *exactly* what she was doing without. She'd have avoided him if she could have, but he was best man to her maid of honor, so ignoring him wasn't an option.

Unfortunately, having sex with him wasn't, either.

Jo Beth had two ironclad rules when it came to sex. She didn't do it close to home. And she didn't do cowboys. Ever.

And, hell, it wasn't as if Clay had ever looked twice at her, anyway. She wasn't the kind of woman a man like him looked at, or even took any particular notice of. She had a decent body—a bit on the skinny side, true, but decent, nonetheless—and she had a nice enough face. Nothing that would stop traffic, but it didn't stop clocks, either. She freely admitted she didn't have enough feminine graces to be what anyone would call beautiful, but she had a certain lean and rangy wholesomeness going for her, an outdoorsy girl-next-door kind of thing that wasn't *completely* unappealing.

Except to men like Clay Madison.

Men like Clay Madison didn't want the wholesome girl-next-door. They wanted flash and sparkle in their women. They wanted curvy bodies, big hair, fluttering eyelashes, and glossy wet-lipped smiles. They wanted adoring, tractable, bosomy, bubble-brained buckle bunnies who gave head at the drop of a trophy belt buckle and didn't make a fuss when the party was over. And they got them. By the truckload. In every town and every city where the rodeo played, the buckle bunnies lined up, waiting for some cowboy to give them a tumble. And if that cowboy happened to be a handsome-assin, four-time Pro Rodeo bull-riding champion with shoulders a yard wide, a tight little butt, and a wicked gleam in his soulful brown eyes, well, that cowboy inevitably got first pick. And it was for certain he would never pick a woman like her.

Not that she'd pick him, either. Not for anything real or permanent. But she sure as hell wouldn't mind having him in her bed. Just once. Just one time to see if he was as good as he looked.

"And, damn, I bet he's fine," she murmured, her eyes drifting closed to better imagine just how it would be.

She pictured herself running her hands over his broad bare shoulders while he kissed her senseless, pictured herself rubbing her bare breasts against his equally bare chest while his hands roamed over her back, pictured herself digging her nails into his firm cowboy butt as he pumped into her. Her mental picture show tightened her nipples inside her plain white cotton bra and had her squirming in the saddle.

Bella tossed her head and looked around to see what was going on.

"Sorry, sweetheart." Jo Beth reached out and patted the mare's neck to reassure her that all was well. Cutting horses and barrel racers took their signals from the movement of the rider in the saddle; a press of the leg just a certain way meant one thing, a shift of weight meant something else. "I didn't mean to confuse you, baby girl."

Dealing with her own confusion was more than enough for the moment.

It wasn't as if she even *liked* cowboys. Well, okay, she liked them all right, as employees, as colleagues, as friends, but definitely not romantically. She'd learned her lesson there the hard way. And, yet, here she was fantasizing about one. Which just proved it was *way* past time she scheduled herself a trip to Dallas for an overdue visit with her favorite cattle broker. Or, maybe, since time was so short and her need was so desperate, she ought to just call up that good ol' boy banker in the next county. He was always real glad to hear from her. Tomorrow, after the wedding, she decided, she'd give Todd a call and see if he'd like to meet her at the Holiday Inn out on Highway 81. A nice sweaty bout of recreational sex was just what she needed to clear her head and settle her nerves so she could concentrate on something besides the physical needs that hadn't been satisfied in far too long. After all, it wouldn't do to be all wound up when the city slickers finally arrived. It might create a bad impression if she bit a paying customer's head off just because that customer was breathing the same air she was.

She shifted in the saddle, arching her back in a long stretch, rolling her head from side to side in an effort to loosen muscles that were tight with tension. In the process, she inadvertently tightened her thighs against the mare's sides. Bella took a quick little sideways jump in response. The move might have unseated a less experienced rider but Jo Beth only swayed in the saddle, keeping her seat without any trouble. "Sorry, Bella," she said again, reaching out to settle the mare with a stroke of her hand.

Hell, she decided, maybe she wouldn't wait until after the wedding to call ol' Todd. He was always real accommodating, always ready to meet her whenever and wherever she wanted him to, always up, as it were, for an afternoon quickie or an all-night marathon. Maybe she'd better call him this afternoon, as soon as she got back to the ranch, and set something up for tonight. Get the kinks out *before* the wedding.

Except, damn it, she couldn't.

Tonight was Cassie's bachelorette party. As maid of honor, Jo Beth was duty bound to show up for it, despite the fact that she was looking forward to it with only marginally less dread than she was to the wedding itself. The difference in her level of enthusiasm being that the wedding would be a public ordeal with everybody in the county in attendance, ready to snicker should she make a fool of herself traipsing down the aisle in a flowing silk dress with rosebuds in her hair.

The bachelorette party, thank God, would at least be a private affair. Silly as all get-out, of course, but blessedly private because the bride had decided she wanted to have an old-fashioned slumber party instead of the more traditional girls' night out on the eve of her wedding. The invitations had specified baby-doll nighties as the preferred wearing apparel for the festivities—"Not in this lifetime," Jo Beth muttered morosely—and they were going to listen to golden oldies, make popcorn balls and ice cream sundaes, and give each other manicures and pedicures so they'd all have matching nail polish for the wedding. As a special surprise for the bride, bridesmaid LaWanda Brewster, who'd recently become an entrepreneur in the at-home sex-toy business, was going to treat them to a demonstration of her most popular products.

Jo Beth shuddered at the mere thought of it, and wondered what it was about weddings that turned otherwise reasonable women into starry-eyed lunatics. Or, hell, maybe it was just her. Maybe she was the lunatic and all the rest of them were behaving perfectly normally under the circumstances. All the other bridesmaids—all five of them—had been tickled pink to be part of the wedding. They'd seemed to genuinely enjoy the shopping trip to Dallas to pick out just the right bridesmaids' dresses, and the endless discussions about the appropriate flowers and which wedding-cake recipe was best and whether the groom's cake should be devil's food or red velvet. They'd been sincerely and utterly delighted with the color-coordinated bridal showers, cooing like doves over the pastel sherbet punch, the platters of tiny crustless sandwiches, and the silly bouquet made out of a paper plate festooned with bows from the shower gifts.

It wasn't that Jo Beth wasn't honored to have been asked to be the maid of honor—after all, she and Cassie had been best friends since kindergarten—but, really, if she had to sit around with a bunch of otherwise rational women and gush over one more precious pot holder with the bride's chosen rooster motif on it, she was going to run screaming from the room.

"Thank God it will all be over tomorrow," she said to Bella as she reined her in and swung out of the saddle.

Her boot heels sent little puffs of dust into the air as they hit the ground, the jinglebobs on her spurs ringing merrily with the movement. She pushed the brim of her hat back with the tip of her index finger and swept her gaze over the empty landscape. A sigh of satisfaction escaped her lips. She'd ridden out into the middle of nowhere—or as close to it as she could get and still be on Diamond J land. In this remote corner of the ranch there was nothing but the hot Texas wind and the land, a few gnarled oak trees that'd managed to stand up to both, and the old wooden windmill, its blades creaking rhythmically above the water tank beneath it.

The tank was made of smooth, weathered concrete and was a foot and a half deep and nearly ten feet across. The water in it was cool and clean. Later in the summer, when the cattle were moved in to graze the pasture, the area around the tank would be thick with mud and the water would be churned up and murky, but right now—at least until the new pool behind the main house was filled—the water tank was the closest thing to a swimming hole on the Diamond J.

And Jo Beth was determined to take full advantage of it.

She looped Bella's reins around one of the crosshatch wooden braces at the base of the windmill, and reached for the metal button on the waistband of her jeans.

WITHOUT LOOKING AWAY from the scene unfolding below him, Clay Madison looped his reins around the saddle horn in front of him, reached into the saddlebag suspended from the rigging behind him, and extracted a pair of high-powered binoculars. Someone was nosing around the water tank in the gully below. It was probably perfectly innocent, just someone intent on getting a drink for themselves or their horse, but it never hurt to make sure. Water was a precious commodity out on the Texas prairie, and a smart rancher took care to safeguard it. Not that Clay was a rancher, but he was the guest of a man who was, and that made it his duty to see what the lone rider messing around down there by the water tank was up to.

Nudging up the brim of his black Resistol cowboy hat with the flick of a finger, he raised the binoculars to his eyes and placed the smooth plastic eyepiece directly against his brow bone. It took a second or two to manipulate the focus wheel, and then, suddenly, with no warning at all, a naked female bottom filled his entire field of vision.

He stared at it for a second or two, then lowered the binoculars, blinked carefully and deliberately, as if to clear an obstruction in his eyes, and repositioned the binoculars. Yep, even at fifty yards there was no mistaking what he was looking at. It was definitely a woman's ass. Creamy white and softly rounded, two perfectly formed globes of luscious female flesh peeked out at him from beneath the hem of a faded blue shirt. As he set there, stock-still atop his borrowed pinto, his gaze fastened unwaveringly on the enticing curves exposed beneath the blue shirt, he was suddenly struck with the overwhelming need to have one burning question answered.

Who's luscious ass was it?

It was nobody he knew or had met in the last inter-minable week, that was for sure. He'd never forget an ass like that. Even if he'd only seen it fully clothed be-fore—and, regrettably, the only asses he'd seen for a couple of months had been fully clothed—he'd have recognized it. It wasn't the kind a man forgot. There was a nice, sweet double handful there, slim enough to en-tice the eye, round enough to give a man something to grab on to when the action got hot and heavy.

But who the hell was it?

He readjusted the focus of the binoculars to take in more of the scene below, telling himself—*promising* himself—he'd watch just long enough to satisfy his cu-riosity about who it was, then he'd turn the pinto around and go back the way he'd come. It was the proper thing, the gentlemanly thing to do. And no matter what certain matrimonially disappointed females might say to the contrary, his dearly departed mama had raised him to be a gentleman. As soon as he knew who it was, he'd go.

Stubbornly, though, almost as if she knew he was there, she kept her back to him as she finished undress-ing. She shrugged out of the blue shirt, letting it slide down her back, covering up her ass for a moment be-fore she caught the shirt by the collar with one hand and reached up to loop it over the saddle horn on top of the pair of jeans already hanging there. Given her size in re-lation to the horse she was using as a clothes rack, she was an inch or two above average height, but she was slightly, almost delicately, built. The waist above that luscious ass was as narrow as a boy's, her arms and legs were sapling slender, and he could clearly see the bumps of her spine, running down the valley of her back like a strand of pearls barely showing beneath her pale creamy skin. The look of fragility was directly countered, however, by the strength inherent in the smooth flex and coil of the well-toned muscles that covered her narrow frame. She was, he decided judiciously, what was commonly called lean and wiry. She looked the way he had always imagined a ballerina would look if you saw her naked. Not his type at all—he preferred exotic dancers to ballerinas—except for that fantastic little caboose.

It gave him hope that what she had in the breast department might be equally fantastic, and had him unconsciously sucking in his breath when she reached up behind her and released the hooks on her plain white bra.

She leaned forward a bit as it loosened, crossing her arms over her torso, lifting her hands to brush the shoulder straps down. As she straightened, reaching out with one hand to stuff the scrap of white fabric into one of the saddlebags strapped to her horse's saddle, she flicked a long brown braid over her shoulder. It was nearly as thick as a man's wrist and came halfway down her back. The sight tickled a memory in Clay's mind. He'd seen a woman with hair like that. Recently, he thought. He was almost sure of it.

But who?

And where?

And then she turned toward him and it seemed as if

his gaze met hers through the precision-ground lenses of the binoculars.

"Jesus," he said, and dropped the binoculars as if they'd suddenly gotten too hot to hold.

It wasn't so much that he thought he'd been discovered. Situated as he was, in a stand of tall cottonwoods and scrub oak just below the crest of a hill, with the hot Texas sun at his back and shining full in her face, it would be almost impossible for her to have seen him. Still, he sucked in his breath and froze for a moment, just in case she had, and wondered what in hell the prissy, dried-up stick of a rancher from the Diamond J was doing shucking her clothes to go skinny-dipping in a watering tank in the middle of the day.

He wouldn't have guessed she had it in her. From what he knew of Miz Jo Beth Jensen—which was, admittedly, not much—she was a serious-minded, no-nonsense, nose-to-the-grindstone kind of woman who seemed to have a perpetual mad-on against men in general and cowboys in particular. What with them both being key members of Cassie and Rooster's wedding party and having similar duties to perform, they'd been thrown together pretty regularly over the last week and he'd read the No Trespassing signs clearly, right from the start.

At their very first meeting, when Rooster had introduced his best man to his bride's maid of honor, Clay had politely dipped his head, touching the brim of his hat with two fingers in the accepted cowboy greeting, and flashed his never-fail "howdy there, darlin'" smile in an effort to start things off on a friendly footing. She'd dipped her head in return and answered his smile with one that could freeze the balls off a prize bull at fifty paces. *Don't even think about it* might as well have been written across her nearly nonexistent chest in bright red letters. He'd done her the courtesy of acceding to her unspoken wishes and hadn't given her another thought that didn't have to do with the wedding preparations.

But that was before he'd seen her standing buck naked in the bright Texas sunlight and realized the dried-up stick of a rancher had one hell of a sweet little body hidden under her dusty jeans and snap-front western shirts. Completely forgetting his vow to leave as soon as he knew who it was, he swung out of the saddle, retrieved the binoculars, and raised them to his eyes.

BRACING A HAND ON THE EDGE of the tank, Jo Beth stepped over the rim and eased into the water. Even warmed as it was by the relentless Texas sun, it still felt deliciously cool against her sun-flushed skin, slick and silky against her thighs and belly, wonderfully refreshing as it lapped against her breasts. She sank down a bit, letting the water slide up over her shoulders and neck to the base of her chin, and tilted her head back so that everything but her face was immersed. And then she sat up and leaned back against the rim of the tank, her eyes closed, her face turned up to the sky, and ordered herself to relax.

It should have been easy. The air was hot and dry and blessedly quiet, the silence broken only by the creaking of the old windmill and the breeze that rustled the leaves of the ancient oak trees that dotted the pasture. The water in the tank was swimming-pool warm. She was completely and utterly alone for the first time in days, her only companion the old horse that stood with her head down and one foreleg bent, drowsing in the shade of the windmill.

And, damn it, she was *still* wound up tighter than an overworked watch spring, and no relief in sight, except what she could give herself. She sat up and smacked the water with the flat of her hand, irritated and annoyed and just plain frustrated that she'd had to resort to her own devices so often lately. Self-love was convenient but she'd never found it all that satisfying. Still, when it was all you had...

She leaned back against the edge of the tank again, closed her eyes, and pressed her hands against her water-slicked breasts, giving in to the fantasy that had been making her crazy for the past week.

CLAY VERY NEARLY DROPPED the binoculars again. She couldn't be doing what it looked like she was doing. Could she? No, prissy, dried-up sticks didn't do that, especially not out in broad daylight in front of God and everybody. Except that she didn't look prissy and dried-up at the moment. She looked luscious and juicy and wanton, lying there in the shallow water with her head thrown back against the rim of the tank and her small, work-worn hands caressing her own breasts. They weren't very large breasts by anybody's reckoning—

certainly not exotic-dancer material—but they weren't nonexistent, either. Small, high and rounded, made buoyant by the water, they were startlingly white under the bright Texas sun, glistening with droplets of water that looked like diamonds on her skin. Her nipples were a pale pinkish-brown, small but beautifully erect, the lighter colored areola drawn up tight and puckered around them. She brushed her fingers across them… back and forth…around and around…slowly, oh-so-slowly…until they were as prominent and deeply pink as the most succulent summer raspberries.

Clay's entire body hardened in response. His jaw clenched. His fingers tightened on the hard plastic casing of the binoculars. His cock swelled in his jeans.

JO BETH PINCHED HER NIPPLES gently, tugging them into hard little points, squirming as she imagined other hands on her aching flesh.

Bigger hands.

Stronger hands.

Clay Madison's hands.

She pictured them in her mind's eye, tanned and calloused, with broad palms and long square-tipped fingers. His nails were clipped and clean, which wasn't always the case with a cowboy. There was a thin, jagged scar across the back of his left hand, the kind a man got from handling barbed wire. Last night at the rehearsal dinner, she'd noted that his right palm bore the dull red marks of a recent rope burn. Hands like that— big, tough, hardworking—would be exquisitely rough against her tender skin. They would envelope her breasts, kneading them, the palms completely encompassing and covering her, making her feel delicate and sexy at the same time. His calloused thumb would rasp against her nipple, moving in slow, maddening circles, around and around, until she was aching and needy, until she couldn't stand it anymore, until she had to have his mouth on her or go crazy.

She arched her back, moaning softly, and let one hand drift down her body to touch the soft, curling hair at the apex of her thighs, while the other stayed where it was, caressing her breasts, plucking at her turgid nipples.

CLAY'S HANDS WERE GRASPING the binoculars so tightly, his fingers very nearly left grooves in the plastic casing. Sweat broke out on his upper lip. Sweet Jesus God! She had her hand between her legs now, touching herself. He couldn't see it beneath the surface of the water because of the sun's glare, but it was obvious what she was doing, obvious how it was making her feel. Her head was pressed back against the edge of the water tank. Her eyes were closed. Her lips were parted. She was panting lightly.

Clay's own breathing increased and his heart started to pound against the wall of his chest, echoing the throbbing behind the fly of his jeans. He could almost taste her…her mouth hot and avid against his…her throat cool and smooth against his tongue…her tight nipples berry-sweet between his lips. He could almost feel her...the strong, slender body arching beneath the weight of his...the slippery softness of her labia against his fingers...the clinging heat and wetness as he pushed them inside her to caress the swollen, weeping walls of her vagina...the hard little nubbin of her clitoris as he circled it with his thumb...her body taut and straining toward his, reaching for fulfillment.

"Oh, baby," he murmured, his voice a low rumble in his throat. "You are *so* hot."

JO BETH FLATTENED HER FINGERS against her mons, applying a firm, kneading pressure, seeing in her mind's eye *his* hand doing the same thing, *his* hand sliding lower, his hand slipping gently into the soft folds between her legs, circling her clitoris with a deft, knowing fingertip. The fantasy was so real now, she could almost feel him next to her, almost feel his mouth on hers, almost feel the brush of his lips against her throat, almost feel his tongue circling her nipples, almost feel his thick, blunt-tipped fingers delving into the slick, swollen passage between her legs, slipping in and out, pressing deep.

She could almost hear his voice in her ear, gravel-rough and whiskey-hot, praising her passion and her firm, slim body, telling her what he wanted from her... telling her what he was going to do to her...telling her how it would feel when he did it.

"Yes." She quickened the movement of her fingers against her clitoris, increasing the pressure, driving herself higher, until she was panting heavily with the need to come, until her body was vibrating with suppressed passion, until every nerve and muscle was taut and tensed, hovering on the maddening edge of release. "Oh, yes," she moaned again and opened her legs wide as if accepting a lover between them. "Yes."

THROUGH THE BINOCULARS, Clay saw her lips move.

"Yes," she said, so clearly he would have sworn he heard the words being whispered in his ear. "Yes. Yes. Oh, yes."

She was almost there. He could feel it as keenly, as sharply, as if he were actually between her wide-open thighs, thrusting into her hot, tight, hungry little pussy. He could feel her body clamping around him, holding on, her legs locked around his waist, her nails digging into his butt, demanding he give it to her.

Harder.

Faster.

Deeper.

In his mind, he was right there beside her…on top of her…inside of her. His heart was slamming against the wall of his chest, his breath was sloughing in and out of his lungs, his whole body was rock-hard and throbbing, aching to give her what she wanted. What they *both* wanted. He struggled to hold on, to hold back, until she reached her peak. A gentleman always let a lady go first, even if only by proxy.

HIS IMAGE FLICKERED behind her closed eyelids, his big hard body moving over her, covering her, his lean horseman's hips settling between her thighs, pushing them wider, his rock-hard cock thrusting into her. She thrust her own hips upward—pistoning, frantic, demanding—but the man of her imagination took over, slowing the pace, deepening the sensation, drawing it out. His movements were measured and deliberate, exactly the way she liked it best, plunging deep into her secret core, withdrawing slowly, plunging again, until she was nearly mad with passion and lust.

Her body arched up out of the water, every sinew stretched tight as she reached for the final crest. Her head rolled against the concrete rim of the water tank. Her fingers worked frantically between her legs. The image in her mind's eye quickened his movements in unison with her mounting need. His hips were pistoning wildly now, too, slamming into hers. His breath was hot against her neck. His big hard hands cupped the cheeks of her ass, lifting her into each hard, driving thrust.

"COME ON, JO BETH," Clay murmured, his voice low and rasping with need. His breathing was in sync with hers. His cock was ready to burst, straining to release the full force of his lust. He held it back by sheer will, waiting for her, coaxing her to the finish with fevered words, wanting it to be as good for her as it was for him. "Come on. Let it go, baby. Let me have it. Give it to me."

"OH, YES. YES," she moaned, and pushed herself over the precipice into the abyss of pure physical sensation. Her whole body clenched tight. "Oh. Clay. *Yes!*"

2

CLAY LOWERED THE BINOCULARS and sagged against the side of his horse, as wrung out and replete as if he'd actually had sex. He'd definitely come, that was for sure. Hands-free and in his jeans, which hadn't happened since he was a hormone-ridden sixteen-year-old making out with Tish Bradley in the front seat of his daddy's pickup. And, incredibly, *this* hands-free orgasm had been hotter and more satisfying than the last time he'd actually come inside a woman.

Of course, the last time he'd come inside a woman, he'd been flat on his back in a hospital bed and buzzed on painkillers, so he hadn't exactly been at his best. Not that the woman in question had voiced any complaints. Quite the contrary. Feeling everything through a haze of pharmaceuticals had muted his physical sensations and slowed his reaction time to the extent that his partner had been limp with blissful exhaustion before he'd joined her at the finish line. She'd been very vocal in her appreciation. So vocal, in fact, that the night nurse had left her desk to see what all the commotion was about. The resulting confrontation, like the amorous encounter that had gone on before it, was kind of fuzzy in his mind. A lot of things had been fuzzy in his mind around that time, starting with the incident that had put him in the hospital bed in the first place.

He'd been stomped by a bull. He knew that because he'd seen the ESPN highlight tape of ol' Boomer dancing on his carcass. Clay didn't actually remember the wreck itself, though, which everybody said was a damned good thing. His last memory of that day—his only memory of the day, really—was walking toward the rodeo office with Rooster to get their competition numbers. Everything else, up to and including his go-round with Boomer, was a complete blank. He knew he'd spent the following three days in intensive care after the doctors finished putting him back together because Rooster had told him he had, but all he recalled of his stay there was a series of shadowy disjointed dreams, the echo of half-heard voices, and vague impressions of worried faces drifting in and out of his field of vision.

By the time he was well enough to be transferred to a regular room, the sequence of his days had gotten clearer and more coherent but they were still kind of fuzzy around the edges, especially in those fog-shrouded minutes just before and after the morphine kicked in.

In the two months since the wreck, the pain had subsided and the pain medication had been changed and decreased, and then changed and decreased again, but his reality had stubbornly remained just the tiniest bit out of focus. He chalked it up to the abrupt and unwelcome modification to his lifestyle. He was used to living fast and hard, traveling from one go-round to the next, always on the move, always on the lookout for the next ride, the next good time, or the next willing woman. Being forced to slow down, even if it was only temporary—and it *was* only temporary—dulled the intensity and blurred the edges, making him, as Rooster was wont to say, a "mite moody."

And then, suddenly, out taking a solitary ride to improve his mood before the bachelor party tonight, everything snapped into sharp focus through the lenses of a pair of borrowed binoculars. For the first time since the wreck, every cell and nerve ending in his body was on red alert, alive and humming and ready to go. And all because he'd watched a woman he barely knew masturbate to climax. A woman, moreover, for whom he hadn't previously spared a second thought—or a second look—beyond what had been required for civility's sake.

Shaking his head at the sheer absurdity of the situation, he tucked the binoculars back into the saddlebag, and mounted up.

He didn't know if it was the surprisingly luscious Miz Jo Beth Jensen herself, or the surprise of coming upon her out of the blue the way he had, or simply the fact that playing the voyeur was something he'd never done before that provided the spark. Whatever it was, he wanted more.

It stood to reason that she wanted more, too. She'd cried out his name when she'd come—he was *almost* sure of it—which meant she had to have been fantasizing about him during that close encounter with her own hand. Clay had been the focus of a good many female fantasies over the years, and he'd found that most women were more than happy to have the chance to make those fantasies real. And, usually, if the circumstances and the woman were right—and sometimes even if they weren't—he'd always been more than happy to oblige.

Completely forgetting that he'd been going to ride away like the gentleman his mama had raised him to be, he clucked softly to his horse and, laying his reins against the side of the pinto's neck, guided the animal out of the trees and down the slope into the gully below, absolutely certain he was about to get lucky.

He kept the horse to a walk and his gaze on the recumbent form of the woman in the water tank. She was leaning back against the concrete edge with her face turned up to the sun and her eyes closed. Her slender, well-toned arms were stretched out to either side of her, resting along the rim of the tank. The position bared her upper body nearly to midtorso, leaving her pretty little breasts resting lightly on the surface of the water. Her whole being reflected complete and utter relaxation.

Clay grinned wickedly. It was a shame, really, to disturb her autoerotic afterglow. But, after all, the woman *had* called out his name in the throes of passion. Hadn't she? And if she hadn't...well, she was obviously in need of what he could do for her. No woman should have to resort to self-manipulation to fulfill her sexual needs, especially not when he was ready, willing and more than able to fulfill them for her.

Watching her as closely as he was, he knew the exact instant she became aware that her solitude was no longer absolute. Her shoulders tensed and she straightened away from the edge of the tank slightly, at the same time sinking down so her breasts disappeared beneath the water just as her rounded knees broke the surface. Surprisingly, she didn't fumble around or scramble to cover herself. She didn't get all fluttery or flustered, either, the way he'd expected her to; the way most other women would have if caught in similar circumstances. She didn't even blush. Instead, she calmly curled one arm around her bent knees and lifted the other, tenting her hand above her eyes in an effort to see who was approaching.

"That's far enough," she said, the unmistakable snap of authority in her voice.

Clay reined in, halting the pinto a good six feet from the edge of the tank, and stared down at her, waiting for what she would do next. It wasn't often a woman managed to surprise him, and she'd done it twice already: first with her heated abandon, then with her complete lack of embarrassment at being caught naked. He couldn't help but wonder what other surprises she had in store for him.

Jo Beth squinted up at him from underneath her raised hand, but all she could see was the silhouetted figure of a man on a horse. His shoulders were impossibly broad against the expanse of blue sky behind him. His face was completely hidden in the shadow of his hat.

Except for the sun glinting off the blunted rowels of his spurs and the silver conchas on his chaps, he was shrouded in darkness.

An instinctive quiver of apprehension snaked its way up Jo Beth's spine. She very deliberately brushed it aside. This was, after all, Diamond J land. She was the jefe of the Diamond J. And he was a Diamond J cowhand.

Whatever reason he might have for trailing her out to this remote corner of the ranch, it sure as hell wasn't because he had any nefarious designs on her body. None of her cowhands would dare. Especially given the mood she'd been in when she left the stable yard.

Which meant there was some problem that demanded her immediate attention back at the main house. Her squint deepened into a frown. Good Lord, couldn't she have one measly hour to herself? Just one measly little hour without the whole operation falling apart?

"This had better be damned important," she said irritably, scowling up at him from under her tented hand.

"Ma'am?"

"Whatever you trailed me out here for. It had better be damned important, or you and whoever sent you out here after me are going to be damned sorry."

"No one sent me after you," Clay said, thinking delightedly that she'd already managed to surprise him again. Whatever he'd expected her to say, however he might have expected her to say it, he certainly hadn't anticipated anything so prosaic as a simple expression of annoyance at his presence and the possible reason for it, especially not with her still sitting there neck deep in water and as naked as the day she was born.

"Then why the hell did you follow me out here?" she demanded.

"I didn't follow you." His easy, affable tone was in direct contrast to the snapping impatience of hers. "I was out taking a ride all by my lonesome and saw someone moving around down here by the water tank." He eased up on the reins as he spoke, letting the pinto amble closer to the concrete tank. "I thought I'd better take a closer look in case that someone was up to no good. So…" Leather creaked as he leaned forward and casually draped a forearm across the saddle horn. The reins dangled loosely from his gloved fingers. The pinto dropped his head and began sucking up water. "Are you up to no good, darlin'?"

Jo Beth opened her mouth to lambaste him for the dual offenses of dereliction of duty and being overly familiar when it occurred to her that not only was he a good deal closer than he'd been a moment before, but— Diamond J cowhand or not—she had absolutely *no* idea who he was.

Nothing about him was familiar. Not the tilt of his hat. Not the sound of his voice. Not even the way he sat his horse. And she prided herself on being able to put a name to every hand on the Diamond J just by watching him ride.

The quiver of apprehension returned, a little stronger this time, a little more insistent as it snaked its way up her spine to lodge at the back of her neck. It wasn't fear.

Not yet. Not by a long shot, she assured herself. But it was close enough to it that she glanced toward Bella, mentally judging the distance to the shotgun holstered behind the saddle, hoping like hell she wasn't going to have to sprint for it, buck naked and dripping wet. Her gaze darted back to the man who seemed, suddenly, to be much too close, much too big, much too…much.

She stiffened her spine against the nascent fear, refusing to give in to it. Her eyes took on a steely glint beneath the shade of her sheltering hand. "Just who the hell are you, cowboy?"

"Beg pardon, ma'am," he said, as polite as if she'd asked a civil question instead of snarling it at him like an angry bobcat. "I didn't realize you didn't recognize me or I'd've made myself known to you straight off." He dipped his head, reaching up to touch two fingers to the brim of his hat. "I'm—"

In that instant, with that slight telling movement, Jo Beth suddenly knew who he was. "Oh, good Lord!" she burst out before she could stop herself. "You're—" She dropped her upraised hand, covering her mouth before the name escaped.

"Clay Madison," he said, and swept his hat off, giving her a theatrical little bow from the saddle. It was the same cocksure, conquering-hero bow he used in the ring to acknowledge the approving roar of the crowd. "In the flesh," he added, with a wickedly charming cowboy grin.

Jo Beth stared up at him for a disbelieving few seconds, her eyes gone wide above her concealing hand, her body frozen like a wild woodland creature trying to escape the notice of a predator. Visions of her fantasies and what she'd done to fulfill them chased round and round in her head. She knew it was too much to hope that he hadn't seen her solo performance. If he'd been watching long enough to see someone moving around *by* the water tank, he'd certainly been watching long enough to have seen what happened after that someone got *in* the water tank.

She closed her eyes briefly, trying to block out the awful reality of the situation, desperately wishing that one or both of them would just disappear into the hot, dry air. But when she opened them again, he was still there, sitting atop the pinto with the sun shining on his gleaming black hair, hat in hand, grinning at her like a feral cousin of the Cheshire cat.

And she was still bare-ass naked, sitting in a water tank in the middle of a sun-baked cow pasture with the guilty blush of self-indulgence heating her cheeks.

There was only one thing to do, one tack to take. She dropped her hand from her mouth, squared her shoulders, lifted her chin, and glared up at him with the expression every hand on her ranch had learned to fear. "Just what the hell are you doing on Diamond J land?"

He shrugged elaborately, unintimidated by the ferocity of her question. "Like I said, I was out taking myself a little ride. Just following my nose, don't 'cha know? Ended up taking the shade in that stand of cottonwoods on the hill, yonder." He gestured with his hat, indicating the gentle swell of the land behind him. "No rhyme or reason to it." His grin flashed again, his eyes raking over her with a warm, appreciative gleam meant to charm and flatter. "Just plain ol' good luck, I'd call it."

"Well, I wouldn't," she snapped, stubbornly refusing to be charmed or flattered. "What I'd call it is plain ol' trespassing. You're on Diamond J land, Mr. Madison, and I'd appreciate it if you'd turn that pinto around and ride back the way you came."

"Well, now, that's not very neighborly." He took a moment to resettle his hat on his head, deliberately thumbing it back a bit so the brim wasn't shadowing his face. "Downright *un*neighborly, I'd say. Especially considering as how I rode down here to see if I could offer you a helping hand." He let his gaze drift downward, away from her face, and his seemingly ever-present grin warmed lasciviously. "So to speak."

Jo Beth tightened her arms around her bent knees and tried not to squirm. "Really?" she said, injecting what she hoped was a credible amount of scorn into her voice.

It wasn't easy.

The man was a living, breathing sexual fantasy. *Her* living, breathing sexual fantasy. She knew as well as she knew her own name that she could have him—right then, right there—just the way she'd imagined in those heated moments of self-induced rapture. All she had to do was say the word and he'd get down off that horse and climb into the water tank with her. She was absolutely sure of it. Just one word, and her frustrations of the last few weeks would come to what was sure to be a glorious end.

But damned if she'd say it.

Fantasy or not, the man was a cowboy. Worse, he was a four-time Pro Rodeo championship bull-riding cowboy. Which meant he was a true wild thing, more reckless, more feckless, more fancy-free and unreliable than the usual breed of cowboy. Trouble with a capital *T,* and she sure as hell didn't need any more of that in her life.

She gave him her haughtiest glare, and tried to think of anything other than what he'd look like soaking wet and wearing nothing but his black Resistol hat. "I thought you rode down here because you saw someone nosing around the water tank and were concerned they were up to no good."

"Yep," he said amiably, wondering exactly what it would take to make her lose her cool and rattle that ironclad composure she wore like a shield. "I surely was. But then I saw you slide down into the water and start...ah..." He hesitated and his gaze dipped downward again, as if he could see beneath the sparkling surface of the water to the place where her hand had been so busily engaged just a few moments ago.

Jo Beth felt every sensitive female part of her body begin to tingle, tensing with anticipation under the promise of that heated look, but she merely smiled—a small, icy, cowboy-withering smile meant to cut a man's ego to ribbons—and raised an imperious eyebrow, daring him to say it flat out.

"Thrashing around in the water like you were doing," he finished smoothly, as if that's what he'd intended to say all along. "Well, it got me to worrying. It surely did.

As far away as I was, there was no telling what kind of trouble you were having."

"Trouble? Is that what you call it?"

The look in his hot-coffee eyes heated to scorching. His wicked cowboy grin turned a shade more knowing and intimate. "Unless you'd like me to call it something else."

Jo Beth ignored the wild leap of her pulse at the invitation implicit in his words and manner. "What I'd *like* is for you to turn around and ride away," she said, knowing she was lying through her teeth. What she'd really like was for him to shuck down to his birthday suit and climb into the water tank with her so she could see if the reality of him lived up to her fantasies.

"And I'd like to oblige you, Miz Jensen," he said genially, lying in his turn. He thumbed the brim of his hat another half inch farther back on his head. "I really would," he said earnestly, as if he actually meant it. "But my dear sainted ma raised me up to be a gentleman like my pa—"

Jo Beth snorted inelegantly.

"—like my pa," he reiterated, giving her a doleful look of mock censure, "an' she'd roll over in her grave for sure if I was to just up and leave you out here by your lonesome, all unprotected and vulnerable-like. Some fella who ain't nearly as well-mannered as me might come along an' try to take advantage of the situation."

The attitude, the words, the tone, the ridiculously thick aw-shucks-ma'am-I'm-just-a-dumb-cowboy accent were all calculated to make him sound as innocent as a wet-behind-the-ears farm boy. Even the way he was wearing his hat, well back on his head with the brim framing his face like a halo, contributed to the impression of a harmless good-natured hayseed bent on doing the right thing.

But the heated look in his eyes, his sly Cheshire-cat grin, even the casual loose-limbed way he sat his horse was a blatant, unabashed sexual come-on, a challenge of the most sexual sort.

I've got what you want, he said, without saying a word. *All you have to do is ask.*

And, oh, it was tempting.

He was tempting.

Too tempting.

And he knew it.

The arrogant jerk.

That's what came of having legions of panting, dewy-eyed buckle bunnies throwing themselves at his feet every time he so much as flashed that lady-killer smile of his. It gave a man an exaggerated impression of his appeal and made him think every woman he met was just dying to get down and dirty with him.

There was only one surefire way to regain her dignity and show him he had absolutely no allure for her.

"Well, then, if you won't leave, I will."

She put her palms on the rim of the tank behind her and pushed herself up. The movement was swift but unhurried, as natural as if she were rising, unobserved, from her bath. And then, using every last bit of self-control she possessed, she stood there for a moment, knee deep in the trough, and calmly, efficiently sluiced water down her arms and torso with the flat of her hands, just as she would have done had she been alone.

That would show him how unimpressed she was with his cowboy charm.

He didn't say a word, didn't so much as move a muscle, but she could feel him watching her, could feel the heat of his gaze following her hands as she briskly skimmed them over her own body. Without looking at him she knew he was completely, absolutely, utterly focused on her. Handsome-as-sin, four-time Pro Rodeo bull-riding champion Clay Madison was looking at *her*. And practically drooling with lust. The sensation was as physical as a touch, as heady as brandy fumes, as irresistible as a soft, sweet kiss in the dark.

Almost without conscious volition, she raised her hands back to her chest, placing her palms flat against her skin, and moved them downward for a second time, outlining the sleek wet lines of her body as she brushed the water from her skin. Her palms slid over the gentle swell of her breasts…caressed the firm, flat plane of her midriff and stomach…brushed ever so lightly across the patch of dark silky hair covering her pubic mound…

He made a strangled sound, something between a moan and a growl.

Jo Beth looked up at him, square into his eyes. What she saw there caused her to cross her hands over her pubic mound, instinctively, as if to hide it from him. But her shoulders remained straight and square, and her chin was well up. "What?" she said belligerently, trying to pretend she wasn't the least bit intimidated.

He didn't move his gaze from her face. "Do you *want* me to climb down off this horse and get into that tank with you?"

For one brief, delicious, insane second, she actually thought about saying yes. What could it hurt, after all? One hot, fast bout of slap-and-tickle with the fantasy cowboy who'd been driving her crazy for the past week might do her some good. It would get him out of her system, relieve the itch, and settle her down for the wedding tomorrow so she could concentrate on her maid-of-honor duties. No one would know. No one would care. And he'd be gone in a couple of days, so it wasn't like she'd be in danger of actually getting involved in any kind of messy public relationship that would need explaining somewhere down the line. She could screw him and forget him, and that would be that.

On the other hand, he had the look of a man who might not be all that easy to forget. And that could be plenty messy in its own way, even if nobody ever found out.

"Well?" he demanded, his glare both furious and fascinated.

She opened her mouth. "Ah…" The word stuck in her throat, and the horror of it was, she didn't know if that word was yes or no. "Ah…"

Clay tightened his hand on the reins, pulling the pinto's nose up and around with one quick twist of his wrist. "Let me know when you make up your mind," he said, and touched his spurs to the horse's sides so that it sprang into a gallop from a standing start.

Jo Beth stood in the water tank, her hands still shielding the dark hair at the top of her thighs, her shoulders still square, and watched him until he disappeared up and over the hill. And then she sank down onto the side of the concrete tank because her knees were trembling too hard to hold her up anymore, and wondered just what the hell she would have said if he'd waited for her answer.

3

"LADIES. LADIES. PLEASE. Let's have a little decorum here." Jo Beth rapped the top of the coffee table with her empty glass. "And another shot. I need to make a toast."

A slender blonde in a hot-pink, lace-trimmed satin chemise peered at her through an untidy fringe of spiky bangs, a half-empty bottle of tequila clutched protectively to her chest. "You just made a toast."

"Well, I'm gonna make another one. I'm the maid of honor. It's my job." Jo Beth rose unsteadily to her knees and thrust her empty glass out across the table, waggling it back and forth under the blonde's nose. "Come on, Roxy. Pour me another shot so I can do my job." She waved her free hand expansively. "Pour everybody another shot."

"Everybody" consisted of all six bridesmaids and the bride-to-be. They were ranged around the glass-topped coffee table in Cassie's living room in various states of dishabille, from Roxy Steele's pink satin and black lace chemise, to Cassie's white eyelet baby doll with embroidered forget-me-not blue flowers, to Jo Beth's yellow cotton knit tank top and green plaid boxer shorts. Thanks to the professional manicurist Roxy had hired as her contribution to the festivities, they all wore Juicy Peach polish on their toenails and sported matching French manicures.

The table was littered with cold slices of half-eaten pizza, barbecued chicken wings and baby back ribs on paper plates, chocolate-smeared sundae glasses, an empty Sara Lee cheesecake box, and a pile of squeezed-out lime wedges. A phallic-shaped saltshaker sat, strategically placed, atop the centerfold of the most recent issue of *Playgirl* magazine.

They'd started the evening with two unopened bottles of Jose Cuervo's finest. The first lay on its side under the table, its contents sacrificed to the evening's merriment. The second bottle was barely half-full.

Roxy obligingly served it up, pouring shots all around. Most of it ended up in the glasses, but some sloshed over onto the table. Not much, though, considering the bartender was halfway sloshed, as well.

Jo Beth bent her head, licking stray drops of tequila off her fingers, then raised her glass and waited until all five of the other bridesmaids—and the bride—had raised theirs, too.

"To Rooster Wills, the groom-to-be." Her tone was somber, her manner solemn and almost respectful, as if she had something of particular gravity to say.

"To Rooster Wills," they echoed, equally somber and serious.

They clinked glasses. More tequila sloshed onto the table.

"May he have more sexual stamina and staying power than the bird he was named after," Jo Beth said and tossed back the content of her glass in one dramatic gulp.

A cacophony of feminine voices erupted in whoops and squeals. Someone giggled. Someone else spewed a mouthful of tequila out of her nose. They had reached the point in the evening's festivities where every utterance seemed screamingly funny to at least half of them, and deeply profound to the rest. They'd also gotten to the point where the discussion of sex was inevitable— and inevitably risqué.

"So how about it, Cassie?" Roxy put her forearm flat on the table for balance and leaned in close, unmindful of the puddles of tequila soaking into the front of her satin chemise. "How is ol' Rooster in the sack?"

Cassie shook her head. "I don't kiss and tell," she muttered, hiding a lopsided smile behind the rim of her glass. "It's not ladylike."

"Aw, come on, Cassie." LaWanda Brewster fluffed her springy red curls in a gesture she'd copied from watching countless old Mae West movies. "There aren't any ladies here. Spill."

"Yeah, spill, Cassie." The added encouragement came from Melissa Meeker, an elegant and urbane mortgage broker who'd flown in from Atlanta the previous evening. "I've always wanted to know if what they say about bull riders is true."

Cassie came out from behind her shot glass and aimed a smile at her old college roommate and sorority sister. "And just what do they say about bull riders?"

"Well." Melissa edged closer to the table and leaned in to dish. Everyone else leaned in, too, until they were huddled over the coffee table like a gaggle of teenaged girls at a slumber party whispering about *S-E-X.* "I don't have any personal experience, you understand. Not like some lucky people I could name—" she rolled her eyes at Cassie, who rolled them right back at her "—but I've heard tell that all that experience riding bulls sort of transfers over into other, more, shall we say, intimate kinds of riding." She waggled her perfectly plucked eyebrows. "If you get my meaning."

They all got it, but, "No, tell us what you mean," La-Wanda said. "Don't be shy. Just lay it right out there on the table."

"I mean," Melissa continued, "if a bull rider can stick on the back of a bull with all that bucking. And twisting." She drew out each word, her voice husky and heated and not the least bit shy. "And thrashing. And heaving. Well, then, it just naturally follows that he'd have that same kind of expertise and stick-to-it-ness in bed. At least—" she sighed lustily "—I sure *hope* it does."

Jo Beth sighed, too, thinking of one particular cowboy bucking and twisting and thrashing around in bed. It created quite a vivid picture in her mind's eye. She sank back down on her heels and crossed her arms, very casually, over her chest in an effort to conceal just how vivid that picture was. Some of the other bridesmaids weren't so circumspect.

"Oh, gawd," LaWanda squealed. "My nipples are getting hard just thinking about it."

"Speaking of nipples…" Barb Kittner, mother of two, heavily pregnant with her third, and the only one of the seven women who hadn't sampled the tequila, smiled dreamily. "Cowboys have great hands. Have y'all noticed that? Big. Strong. Capable." Her dreamy smile turned a shade sly as she pinched her own nipples through the fabric of her soft cotton nightshirt. "Talented."

The other women hooted in approval.

Jo Beth pressed her thighs together and tried not to think of Clay Madison's hands and what she had imagined them doing to her earlier that afternoon. Tried not to think of what they would most certainly have done if she'd invited him into the water tank with her instead of sending him away. If she'd said yes, if she'd actually allowed him to do everything she'd *imagined* him doing, she wouldn't be suffering the tortures of the foolishly celibate now, listening to the other women talk about cowboys' legendary—and wholly inflated!—sexual expertise.

"They've got great butts, too. Nice and small with tight, compact little buns. Tasty." Karen Holden, oldest bridesmaid by six months and leader of the Bowie First Fellowship Church Choir, smacked her lips. "Mighty tasty." She chuckled wickedly. "Makes me want to leave teeth marks on 'em."

"Good idea." LaWanda waved her empty glass to show her approval. "Put your brand right smack-dab on their cute little tushies. Keep 'em from straying."

Jo Beth pressed her thighs even tighter together, and prayed for a turn in the conversation. Good Lord! Did all women have the same fantasies about cowboys? Or had she somehow telegraphed her lustful daydreams to the rest of the bridesmaids? Not that she'd actually imagined biting Clay's backside but…damn if the idea didn't sound kind of appealing, now that she thought of it. She squirmed slightly, trying to banish the picture of Clay lying facedown in the sheets on her bed, his tight little cowboy butt offered up like a particularly tasty treat.

"They've got great shoulders, too," Melissa said. "Have you noticed? You just don't see any stoop-shouldered cowboys running around, now do you? I wonder why that is?"

An instant picture formed in Jo Beth's mind of Clay Madison's shoulders. They were a yard wide, at least. Or they'd looked that wide, at any rate, with him sitting up there, atop that pinto gelding, with the sun at his back, silhouetting his impressive shoulders against the blue sky. They'd have been more impressive, of course, without the shirt. Jo Beth closed her eyes, imagining it…imagining him slowly unsnapping the front of that black shirt…imagining him sliding it down off one magnificently broad shoulder…imagining…

"I just like the way cowboys are built. Period," La-Wanda said. "All lean and wiry, with— Hey, Jo Beth. You falling asleep on us?"

Jo Beth's eyes snapped open. "Oh. No. Sorry. Just resting my eyes. Too much tequila," she said, flushing as she pushed her empty glass away. "I need to switch to something softer." She placed one hand flat against the table and levered herself to her feet. "Anybody else want a Coke or a Dr. Pepper while I'm up?"

Nobody did.

They refilled their shot glasses with what was left of the tequila and went right on talking about cowboys while she made her way out to the kitchen.

THINGS WERE A TAD MORE SEDATE over in the bunkhouse at Tom Steele's Second Chance Ranch, where Rooster and his groomsmen were holding the bachelor party. The seven men sat around a scarred wooden game table, mostly silent as they scrutinized the cards they'd been dealt. George Strait sang softly from the CD player. A narrow side table held the remains of a jumbo deli platter. The yeasty smell of beer mixed with the cigar smoke hovering in a blue cloud over their heads.

"I'm in." Clay tossed a couple of chips into the pot in the middle of the table, then reached out a long arm and tapped his cigar on the edge of a terra-cotta flowerpot they were using as an ashtray. So far, the spiny barrel cactus in it didn't seem any the worse for wear. "So, what are the ladies up to tonight?"

Rooster squinted at the cards in his hand. "Slumber party," he said and tossed in his chips to match Clay's bet.

"Slumber party?"

"Yeah, you know. A bunch of women in pajamas doin' girl stuff. Watchin' sappy movies. Eatin' popcorn. Talkin' about whatever it is women talk about when they get together. Probably fixin' each other's hair and nails. Stuff like that."

Clay immediately honed in on what was really important. "What kind of pajamas?"

Tom grinned around the thin black cheroot clamped in his teeth. "I can't speak for the rest of them, but Roxy packed a really hot-looking pink number with lace all over it," he said. He'd been jealous of Clay once, a long time ago. He figured it was only fair Clay return the favor now. "Black lace."

"Black lace, huh?" Clay threw down a couple of cards. "Two," he said to Hector before turning to Rooster. "How 'bout Cassie?"

Rooster was still squinting at his cards. "How 'bout Cassie what?"

"Her pajamas. She pack a hot number for the slumber party, too?"

"Cassie don't wear pajamas," Rooster said, and then blushed beet-red. "What I mean is," he sputtered, manfully ignoring the snickering of his groomsmen, "she wears a nightgown."

"What color?" Clay asked.

"I dunno. Blue, usually."

"It have any lace on it?"

Rooster shook his head. "Flowers," he said, as he tossed down a single card and signaled for one to replace it.

Quiet reigned for a moment as they all studied their newly reconstituted hands. Bob Evers and Tiny O'Leary, both buddies of Rooster's from the rodeo circuit, threw down their cards in disgust and got up to get more beer and scavenge at the remains of the deli platter. The other five men all added chips to the pot.

"You know who I wouldn't mind seeing in her pajamas is that redhead," Tiny said as he wandered back to the poker table to kibitz. He had a fat dill pickle in one hand and a beer in the other. "That LaWanda what's-her-name?"

"LaWanda Brewster," Rooster said.

"Yeah, that's the one." Pickle juice dripped down onto the front of Tiny's plaid shirt but he paid it no mind. "She's built real nice, that one is. I bet she looks fine in her pajamas. Or in nothin' at all, if it come to that."

"Well, hell, if we're fantasizin' here and pickin' favorites, I'll admit to some curiosity about that slick little gal who flew in from Atlanta yesterday." Joel Boyd, who ran the local feed store, had been a friend of Rooster's since they both got sent to detention in high school. "I bet she wears one of those thong things. Most city women do."

"And you'd know that how?" Tom said. He'd known Joel since high school, too, and felt free to razz him when the BS quotient got too high.

"I read about it in *Cosmo*," Joel said, deadpan. He tossed a chip into the pot. "Call."

Rooster grunted derisively. "I think you'd be ashamed to admit you read that kind of smut." He tossed in two chips, doubling the bet. "Call and raise."

"I'm out." Tom laid his cards facedown on the table and reached for his beer. "You know, I saw all Cassie's bridesmaids in their pajamas once," he said into the silence, as they waited for Clay to decide whether he was in or out. "Briefly. It was back in high school. Me and Rooster and a couple of our buddies got it into our heads to crash the cheerleaders' annual slumber party."

Rooster smiled in fond remembrance. "The girls

started screamin' and runnin' around like a bunch of chickens with their heads cut off when we tapped on the window glass. You'd'a thought we was serial killers or somethin'. A right fine sight, it was. All those cheerleaders flittin' around in their baby-doll nightgowns."

Clay glanced up from his contemplation of his cards. "Any of 'em wearing lace?"

"Not that I recall." Tom finished off the last swallow of his beer and flipped the empty can into a wastebasket. "'Course I have to admit I was kind of distracted by LaWanda's sister. She's seven or eight years older, which would have made her all of about twenty-four at the time. She was chaperoning the party." He shot a grin at Rooster. "Remember?"

Rooster gave a bark of laughter. "I ain't likely to forget it. She came chargin' out onto the porch with her daddy's shotgun pumped and ready, wearin' nothin' but a skimpy little black nightgown—"

"With lace," Tom added for Clay's benefit.

"—and her hair done up with them big pink rollers with one of those what'd'ya call 'em?—beauty masks?—smeared all over her face. Threatened to pepper our asses with buckshot if we didn't hightail it outta there. She would'a done it, too."

"She a redhead, too?" Tiny took up the subject of LaWanda and redheads as if they'd never left it. "I've always been partial to red hair on a woman. Top and bottom, if you know what I mean."

"Gentlemen, please." Hector "Padre" Menendez censored them all with a look from beneath his grizzled brows. He was an imposing patriarchal figure, more than twice the age of most of the other groomsmen, and had had a hand in raising both Rooster and Tom. "You're talking about our friends and neighbors, and the wives and daughters of our friends and neighbors. Show a little respect."

They all had the grace to look shamefaced, except Clay, who sat brooding at his cards, wondering why no one had picked Jo Beth Jensen as an object of their erotic fantasies. True, she wasn't as out-and-out, in-your-face sexy as Tom's wife Roxy. She didn't have flaming red hair and generous curves like LaWanda. She lacked Cassie's kittenish cuteness. But, damn, she was *hot*—burning-up-the-stove, curl-your-toes, fry-your-brain hot.

Hadn't any of these jackasses ever *looked* at her, he wondered, forgetting that he himself hadn't really looked at her, either, until she appeared naked in the viewfinder of his binoculars.

"Hey, pard." Rooster nudged him with his elbow. "You gonna hold 'em or fold 'em?"

"Sorry." Clay tossed in the chips necessary to stay in the game. "Hold," he said, and then sat silently while the game progressed, entertaining himself with fantasies of Jo Beth Jensen wearing nothing but a black-lace thong while performing lewd and wonderful acts upon his body.

It was a shame, really, that he wouldn't be in town long enough to make those fantasies a reality. On the other hand, he wasn't planning to leave Bowie until the day after the wedding. Two days was more than enough time to make his fantasies—and hers—come true.

"Well, hell, if you're gonna sit there grinnin' like a skunk eatin' cabbage, I'm out, too," Rooster said, and tossed down his cards.

THEY WERE STILL TALKING about cowboys when Jo Beth came back into the living room with an icy can of soda in her hand.

"It's not just that they have the…um…bucking technique down pat," Roxy was saying as Jo Beth carefully folded herself back down between the coffee table and sofa. "Or how great their hands and butts are. It's their incredible stamina. That's what *really* impressive."

Melissa's gulp was audible. She licked her lips. "They have incredible stamina?"

"Oh, yeah." Roxy nodded sagely. "In-cred-i-ble. And it's not just bull riders. It's bronc riders, too. Think about it. They're in the saddle, on top of those bulls and broncs, day after day. Sometimes two and three times a day during the summer season. And night after night, too. Isn't that right, Cassie?"

Cassie nodded so hard she nearly toppled over.

"For a bull or bronc rider the job is all about holding tight and staying on till the ride's over. That's the cowboy way. And they tend to keep right on doing it that way." Roxy flashed a wickedly smug little smile. After all, her husband had been a champion bronc rider. "Even after they retire."

Jo Beth snorted derisively, deciding it was time to in-ject a little reality into the conversation. They could *all* use a dose of common sense to counter the braggado- cio. And she could certainly do with a change of sub- ject. All this talk of cowboys and sex was getting her hot. Okay, hotter.

"Cowboys may stay on till the ride's over," she said, "but in rodeo, remember, the ride's over in eight seconds."

"Yeah, but it's a wild ride," Cassie said. "And they're *always* ready for a second and third go-round to better their score."

Roxy hoisted her empty glass. "To the cowboy way!"

The other women whooped and hollered.

Jo Beth pressed the cold soda can to the pulsing vein in her neck to cool herself down. It didn't help.

"WELL, BOYS, I think I'll call it a night." Hector rose stiffly from his seat, mindful of the arthritis that stiff- ened his joints when he sat in one position for too long. "I'm not as young as I used to be, and sunup seems to come earlier every day."

"I think I'll chuck it in, too," Joel said. "I promised Margie I wouldn't stay out too late."

"Since when is ten o'clock late?" Tiny asked.

"Since Joel Jr. started teething and Margie started having her morning sickness at night."

"Well, if that don't beat all." Tiny shook his head in disbelief. "Breakin' up a perfectly good poker game be- cause of a cranky baby and a woman who can't keep her supper down." He leveled a half-humorous, half-serious glance at Rooster. "That's what happens when you get married, you know. You sure you wanna go through with it?"

"Sure as death and taxes."

"Well, don't say nobody warned you." Tiny pushed to his feet. "See y'all tomorrow at the church." He cuffed Rooster on the shoulder as he rose. "'Less you come to your senses before then, that is."

"Hey, the game don't have to break up just because Hector and Joel are out," Rooster protested. "Five players is more than plenty to keep it interestin'."

"Naw, I think I'll head back to the motel and hit the sack. I'm kinda tired now that I think on it." Tiny yawned hugely. "And my luck ain't been all that good tonight, anyway." He nudged Bob Evers with the toe of his boot. "You 'bout ready to roll?"

"Yeah, sure." Bob lumbered to his feet. "You own the keys to the truck."

"They ain't goin' to the motel no how, no way," said Rooster as the door to the bunkhouse swung closed behind his two escaping groomsmen. "Tiny O'Leary ain't never hit the sack before midnight for as long as I've known him, unless he had a woman in it with him. They're headin' over to that honky-tonk out on 81. They got strippers there."

"I thought about getting strippers for tonight," Clay said. "Bachelor party tradition an' all, you know? But, then, I decided against it because, well, hell." He shrugged. "I figured Cassie and the rest of the ladies wouldn't like it if they found out we'd had strippers." It was the truth, as far as it went, just not the whole truth.

The whole truth was that he'd kind of lost his taste for that sort of thing even before the run-in with ol' Boomer had put a crimp in his love life. But that wasn't the kind of thing one man admitted to another—especially when that man had a reputation to protect. "We could head over to the honky-tonk if you want to, though. It's your bachelor party."

Rooster thought about it for a second or two. "Naw." He shook his head. "You're right. The ladies wouldn't like it none."

"OH. MY. GOD." Cassie shrieked and hid her face in a fringed throw pillow as the male stripper yanked off his tear-away pants and started gyrating in front of her wearing only a black satin jockstrap, fringed chaps and cowboy boots.

"Don't you pay her no mind, darlin'," LaWanda hollered encouragingly when Cassie refused to take his hand and join him on the floor. "You just swivel them hips right on over here to me. I'll dance with you." She grabbed Jo Beth by the hand and pulled her to her feet. "We'll both dance with you."

Jo Beth considered refusing for about two seconds. "Oh, what the hell," she said, throwing caution to the wind. She'd had just enough alcohol not to be appalled at the up-close-and-personal sight of the bare buttocks of a complete stranger. "Why not?"

It was, after all, the closest she'd been to a nearly naked male body in some time. Given the way things were going, it might be the closest she'd get for some time to come. She put her hands on his hips, just above the low-slung waistband of his chaps and plastered herself to his back. LaWanda came at him from the front. Thus sandwiched together, they began to bump and grind their way around Cassie's living room to vintage Hank Williams Jr. belting out "Honky Tonk Women" at full volume.

It wasn't long before every woman in the room, including the blushing bride-to-be, had joined the love train.

"THIS IS DOWNRIGHT PITIFUL. Y'all know that don't you?" Tom sat with his chair tilted back on two legs. His booted feet, crossed at the ankles, rested on the edge of the game table. A can of beer was balanced on his upraised knee. "Three grown men who can't think of anything better to do at a bachelor party than sit around drinking beer and watching rodeo on ESPN."

His comment brought no response from the other two men. Their attention was focused squarely on the bull-riding action taking place on the big-screen TV.

"See there?" Clay gestured at the screen with his beer. "See how that Taylor kid uses his spurs on the downswing?"

"Yep, I see." Rooster nodded in acknowledgment. "Reminds me of another young bull rider I know once."

"It damned well should," Clay said, trying not to sound as disgruntled as he felt. "The kid told me right out loud that he copied that move by watching slow-motion tapes of me in action."

"There ain't no disgrace in that. You did the same

yourself, once upon a time. So'd I. So'd Tom. So'd every professional cowboy out there who's worth his salt. It's the best way to learn aside from doin' it."

"Yeah, well." Clay took a sip of his beer to avoid saying any more. Rooster was right. There was no disgrace in watching and learning from a competitor's tapes; it was standard practice for professional athletes in every sport. But, hell, there was just something about the young bull rider currently strutting his stuff on the TV screen that rubbed Clay the wrong way. The kid was too cocky by half, for one thing. And he wasn't near as good as he thought he was—a fact that would be amply illustrated when Clay was healed up enough to return to the circuit.

"Judgin' by the way he's movin' up in the rankings, he appears to be learnin' right well," Rooster said.

"That'll slow down some when he gets some real competition."

"Meanin' what?"

"Meaning the two top contenders for the last four years running aren't competing this year due to injuries and—"

"That'd be you and Marty Bates."

"That's right. Me and Marty Bates. Plus Bud Taggart's been slowed down considerably by his bad back, so his scores aren't near as high as they should be. It's probably his last year on the circuit, if his wife doesn't nag him into quitting before the season's over." He could feel the tension ratchet up inside him as he spoke, all out of proportion to the subject at hand, and had to make a concerted effort to keep his tone even. "But Marty will be out of his cast in another couple of weeks, and I'll be back on the circuit next year. Then we'll see how fast that Taylor kid moves up the rankings."

"I thought the doctors told you not to plan on goin' back on the circuit," Rooster said.

The sudden wave of anger and anxiety that washed over Clay at his friend's words took him by complete surprise. He had to clamp down hard—physically and emotionally—to keep from showing it.

"What the hell do doctors know?" he said, waving a hand dismissively. Casually. He *had* to be casual. "They told me I wouldn't be back after that wreck in Abilene six years ago when I cracked those two bones in my back, either. Or the time I got kicked in the head and was unconscious for three days. They were wrong then. They're wrong now."

But Rooster wouldn't let it go. "You were a lot younger then. Broken bones and broken heads heal faster when you're young."

"All that means is it'll just take me a little longer to heal this time. It doesn't mean I won't go back."

"It means you shouldn't, though."

"Leave it alone, Rooster."

"I'm only just sayin'—"

"Leave it alone," Clay said, more sharply than he had intended.

Tom tsk-tsked loudly. "Just plain downright pitiful." He shook his head with mock ruefulness. "They ought to just take the three of us out and shoot us."

"What the hell are you bellyachin' about?" Rooster said, turning to the man who had been his first partner on the rodeo circuit, way back before he up and married a blond firecracker named Roxy.

"It's your bachelor party. Your last night on earth as a free man. And the three of us are sitting here, watching the TV, like tired old coots in a nursing home."

"We could crash the slumber party," Clay suggested, thankful for the change in conversation. He didn't want to discuss his return to rodeo with Rooster. He didn't like how it made him feel, and it wasn't a subject that was open for discussion, anyway. "Reenact a memorable event from your ill-spent youth."

"Well, now, there's a thought," Tom said, as if he were actually considering it. "What do you think, Rooster? Care to take a stroll down memory lane? Go tapping on the window glass in the dark of night and give the ladies a thrill?"

"Lord, no! Them ladies is a lot meaner now than they was back in high school. We'd have all of 'em out on the porch with shotguns this time."

"Yeah, but it might be worth it to see the whole bevy of 'em in their pajamas again. Like old times." Tom grinned. "Besides, none of them can shoot worth a damn anyway, so we wouldn't be in all that much danger."

"You're forgettin' about Jo Beth. She could shoot the fleas off a dog without partin' its fur." Rooster's smile was just a tad bit sly. "And she's a damned sight more likely to take aim at you than she would some flea-ridden hound."

Clay sat up a little straighter in his chair. "What's Jo Beth got against you?"

"Nothing," Tom said quickly. Too quickly. "And it happened years ago, anyway. It's water under the bridge."

"*What's* water under the bridge?"

"Tom here broke his engagement to Jo Beth when he met Roxy," Rooster said, more than happy to provide the information.

"I was never engaged to Jo Beth."

"Not officially, maybe. But everybody knows you was fixin' to pop the question at the end of the rodeo season. You would've, too, if you hadn't met up with Roxy in that honky-tonk in Lubbock. You should remember how they met up, Clay. You was there. It was your first season on the circuit."

"I remember it very well." Clay cut a deliberately reproachful glance at Tom. "I didn't know he was engaged to Jo Beth while he was sparkin' Roxy, though. I bet she didn't know it, either. It's not the kind of thing she'd put up with."

"Gawddammit," Tom said. "I was *not* engaged to Jo Beth."

"Near as makes no difference," Rooster insisted, gleefully sticking the needle in. "The shame of losin' you is what soured that little gal on cowboys and turned her into a bitter old maid."

"Oh, for cryin' out loud. You're as gossipy as an old maid yourself." Tom dropped his feet to the floor. "You two can stay up swapping lies all night, if you want, but I'm going to bed."

Rooster snickered. "'Pears he's a mite touchy on the subject."

"Appears so," Clay agreed.

The last two men left on the field grinned at each other in mutual understanding and perfect harmony. There were few things more satisfying than successfully tweaking a good friend about his past.

"Is she really a bitter old maid?" Clay asked.

"Oh, hell, no. I just said that to yank ol' Tom's chain."

"She soured on cowboys?"

"Well." Rooster shrugged. "She ain't had any truck with one since Tom throwed her over for that firecracker he married. Why? You got interests in that direction?"

Clay shrugged noncommittally. "She's a woman, isn't she?"

"Well, there's women and there's women. And she ain't like any woman you ever known before."

"Meaning what?"

"Meaning she ain't a buckle bunny out lookin' for a good time, is what. She's a rancher. And that means she's hard-headed and ornery and more prideful than most folks here 'bouts think is becomin' in a female."

"But she's still a woman."

"Can't argue with that," Rooster conceded and, having reached his quota of conversation for the evening, turned his attention back to the action on the TV screen.

The next fifteen minutes were filled mostly with companionable silence and the occasional rhetorical comment about some bull rider's performance, or lack thereof. Finally, when the credits started to roll, Clay stood up.

"Well, pard, unless you have a hankering to head on over to that girlie bar, after all, it looks like your bachelor party is officially over."

"Looks like," Rooster agreed, and got to his feet as well. "See you in the mornin'."

Less than fifteen minutes later, Clay found himself alone in bed, staring up at the moonlight and shadows on the ceiling, with nothing else to do but lie there remembering every delicious detail of Jo Beth Jensen's wet, naked body—and every nuance of his response to it. It was a long time before he went to sleep.

THE PARTY WAS STILL GOING strong over at Cassie's. At eleven o'clock—while Clay was busy with his party of one—the ladies trooped out, en masse, onto the porch to wave the stripper on his merry way, then trooped back inside to play X-rated bachelorette party games with X-rated prizes thoughtfully provided by LaWanda from the inventory of her new at-home sex-toy business.

At midnight, they discovered that Melissa Meeker was the first to succumb to too much revelry. "Jet lag," Cassie said kindly, as she draped a knitted afghan over the recumbent form of her sorority sister.

Barb Kittner went down thirty minutes later. "Come on, honey," Roxy said to the mother-to-be. "Let's get you into a bed before you fall asleep on your feet."

By one-fifteen, only Jo Beth and Cassie were left awake, with the less stalwart members of the bride's entourage sleeping all around them.

"I'll tell you one thing," Jo Beth said, as she attempted to smooth out the lumps in her sleeping bag. "It's a damned good thing the wedding isn't until four o'clock tomorrow. Any earlier and some of your bridesmaids would still be too hung over to make it."

Cassie yawned hugely and snuggled deeper into her pillow. "It was a great party. Thanks for doing it for me."

"You're welcome, sweetie. But it wasn't just me, you know." She slipped her hand under the sleeping bag, intent on finding the source of her discomfort. "Everyone help— Good God, what's this thing?"

Cassie peered at the tangled web of straps and buckles dangling from Jo Beth's fingers through eyes made heavy by too little sleep and too much tequila. "I think LaWanda called that a bondage harness."

"What the hell do you do with it? No, don't tell me. I don't want to know." She dropped it on the coffee table next to a feathered wand, a jar of edible body paint, a far too realistically shaped purple latex vibrator, and a battery-operated device called Kitten Klamps, which looked like miniature jumper cables and was meant—if she recalled LaWanda's explanation correctly—to be attached to various delicate areas of a woman's anatomy. "Do you believe people actually *use* this stuff?"

A delicate snore was her only answer.

The bachelorette party was officially over.

Jo Beth punched her pillow into a more comfortable position, snuggled down into her sleeping bag, closed her eyes…and dreamed heated dreams involving Clay Madison, body paint, and jumper cables. It was not a restful slumber.

4

DESPITE THE FACT that two of the bridesmaids started out the day with massive hangovers, and one of the grooms-men was sporting a doozy of a black eye, the wedding was a joyous affair and went off without a hitch to mar the solemnity and beauty of the festivities. If Jo Beth hadn't had to share duties that kept her practically joined at the hip with Clay, she would have enjoyed it unreserv-edly. As it was, her nerves were stretched almost to the limits of her self-control by his unalleviated, unrelent-ing, *unsettling* presence.

He was there when she arrived at the Bowie First Fel-lowship Church, standing in the wide arched doorway at the top of the stairs in a classic tuxedo and shiny black cowboy boots with all the other identically clad groomsmen who, somehow, seemed to fade into insig-nificance next to all the effortlessly gorgeous in-your-face masculinity that was Clay Madison. She could feel his eyes on her, watching silently, a slight sly smile curving his lips as she and the other bridesmaids shep-herded the flustered and fluttering Cassie out of the limo and up the stairs into the vestibule that had been set aside for the female members of the wedding party. She kept her head averted and her chin lifted, pretending she was too preoccupied with keeping the lavishly embroidered train of the bride's billowing white dress from dragging on the steps to notice his presence.

He was there at the pulpit beside Rooster, standing easily, shoulders squared, feet slightly apart, his big hands clasped loosely in front of him as the processional played. That same slight smile hovered around his lips and a knowing, salacious gleam was in his hot-coffee eyes as he watched her precede Cassie down the aisle. She stared past him, hands tight around her bouquet of peach-colored Sunset Celebration tea roses, which matched the silk dresses she and the other bridesmaids wore. Fastening her gaze oh-so-reverently on the stained-glass window that graced the sanctuary's rear wall, she mentally counted her steps and hoped to hell she didn't stumble in her strappy dyed-to-match high-heeled sandals.

He was there at the ceremony's end, hovering with what felt like considerably more than appropriate attentiveness, his elbow crooked to receive her hand for the recessional when it came time to make their way back down the aisle behind the beaming bride and groom. She accepted his arm with a vague smile meant to convey to him just how inconsequential he was to her except as an officially sanctioned escort, and pretended not to notice the rock-hard firmness of the muscles beneath the smooth black fabric under her palm.

He was there, squished between LaWanda Brewster

and Melissa Meeker—who, she noted sourly, made absolutely *no* attempt to give him any breathing room—in the back of one of the two white stretch limousines hired to transport the wedding party to the Second Chance Ranch for the reception. She ignored the fact that they were sitting practically knee to knee in the crowded interior and focused all of her considerable attention on making Tiny O'Leary believe his animated account of the barroom brawl he'd been in at a honky-tonk out on Highway 81 the night before was utterly fascinating.

He was there during the interminable picture-taking with the official wedding photographer before the reception began, flirting with the bridesmaids, keeping the groomsmen loose, and making Cassie—and Rooster—blush for the camera. She smiled on cue and ignored him as if he were invisible, refusing to be taken by his good-natured, good-ol'-boy act.

He was there, standing next to her in the receiving line at the official start of the reception, greeting Cassie and Rooster's guests with a mixture of easygoing charm and effortless efficiency that made them feel welcome without inviting them to linger and hold up the line. She assured everyone of her pleasure in seeing them, and ignored the heat that sizzled up her arm every time she and Clay inadvertently bumped elbows.

He was there, sitting next to her at the linen-covered head table while the wedding supper was served and eaten. She chatted vivaciously with Hector Menendez, who sat on her other side and Bill Evers who sat across from her, and pretended to ignore the outrageous way Clay flirted with every bridesmaid except her.

And he was there when the bride and groom invited the wedding party out onto the dance floor to join them at the conclusion of their first dance as husband and wife. Rising to his feet beside her, he held out his hand—his big, calloused hand, with the rope burn across the palm—and practically dared her not to take it.

"I believe this is our dance, Miz Jensen," he said politely, leaving her no option but to stand up with him or have everyone in town gossiping for the next two months about how the maid of honor at Cassie and Rooster's wedding had been so rude as to refuse to dance with the best man.

She'd been the focus of quite enough gossip in her life concerning her relationships—or lack thereof—with cowboys. She didn't want to be at the center of any more.

Without a word, she put her hand in his and let him lead her onto the floor. As he swung her into a lively country two-step, Jo Beth discovered it was impossible to ignore him any longer.

The man she'd been fantasizing about for the last week was holding her in his arms as they revolved around the dance floor. The hard, muscled chest she had imagined pressed against her bare breasts was less than a foot away, covered only by the fine pin-tuck pleating on the front of his white cotton dress shirt. The hands she'd envisioned stroking her naked, needy body were warm against her all-too-receptive flesh, touching her lightly at shoulder and palm. The sculpted lips she had pictured ravishing hers were within kissing distance, curved upward at the corners in the slight, sly smile that made her want to sink her teeth into his lush bottom lip. He radiated strength and heat and sheer masculine sex appeal. And he danced—there was no other word for it—divinely, with a strong, sure lead and a lazy swaying rhythm that had the fluttering handkerchief hem of her peach silk bridesmaid's dress brushing against the black gabardine fabric of his tuxedo trousers with every supple turn and twist of their bodies. She couldn't help but wonder if he'd exhibit the same control and rhythm in bed.

She could feel her temperature rising in response to having all that magnificent masculinity so temptingly, teasingly near. She could feel her body tingling…her breasts tightening…her thighs softening…her resistance melting like butter in the hot Texas sun.

"Well, hell," she muttered, thoroughly disgusted with her inability to control her lust around this totally unsuitable man, this…this *cowboy*.

He chuckled wickedly, knowingly, and executed a tricky little dance step that brought her six inches closer. His hand shifted on her bare shoulder, moving to cradle the curve of her neck. His fingertips pressed ever so lightly against her sensitive nape. His thumb brushed ever so softly against the hollow at the base of her throat. He brought their clasped hands closer in to their sides so that the back of his brushed against her thigh with every swaying step they took.

Heat flooded through her in a wild torrent, unlike anything she had ever felt before. It was all she could do not to turn her cheek against his caressing hand and rub against it like a cat in heat, demanding to be petted and stroked. She swallowed convulsively, ruthlessly tamping down the urge, and managed to retain her dignity. No one watching them would see anything beyond a formally attired couple pirouetting in approved country style to a sprightly country two-step. No one would know how desperately she wanted to close that yawning six-inch gap between them…to press her breasts to his chest…to crush her lips to his…to give in to the wild sexual impulses surging through her.

He knew, though. He spun her lightly out and away from him, guiding her back so she twirled under his raised arm in a showy move that ended with her pressed against the hard length of his body. Her lips were within inches of his. Her spine was bowed in a graceful arc. Their clasped hands were tight against the small of her back, pressing her lower body against his.

It was a maneuver he'd perfected on countless dance floors in countless honky-tonks with countless adoring buckle bunnies. It always turned them to putty in his hands. He had no doubt it would work the same magic on Jo Beth Jensen.

She glared up at him through the fringe of her lashes, her lips pursed, her body tense, her senses humming with anticipation and temper and pure unadulterated lust.

God, he was gorgeous.

And sexy.

And cocky as hell.

That last should have turned her off. If she had the sense God gave a goose, it *would* have turned her off. Unfortunately, it only made her hotter.

There was really no sense fighting it.

She lifted her lashes, looked directly into his wicked brown eyes, and smiled invitingly.

He flashed her a lazy, ain't-I-irresistible grin. "Decided not to be mad at me, after all?" he said, and dipped her slightly, so that her head fell back into the cradle of his hand and she was forced to tighten her grip on his lean waist to keep her balance. Their lower bodies were pressed more tightly together than before. He swiveled his hips, just slightly, making sure she felt what he wanted her to feel, imposing himself on her with the unmistakable, unsubtle body language of the dominant male animal intent on staking a claim.

"No, actually—" she held the position for a heartbeat, returning the pressure of his hips with the answering pressure of her own, her gaze locked with his, unabashed and uncowed, letting him know she wasn't the least bit intimidated by his show of masculine dominance "—what I've decided to do is fuck you."

To Jo Beth's unalloyed pleasure, his cocky grin faded and his face went utterly blank with something that looked very much like shock. He brought her upright with the hand at the back of her head, moving her smoothly, effortlessly into the next step of the dance. They took two quick whirling turns around the dance floor in complete silence while Clay considered what she'd said.

He didn't know why he was so taken aback by it. He knew she wanted to have sex with him—hell, most women did!—so it wasn't as if what she'd said came as any big surprise. And he'd certainly heard the word before, and said it any number of times himself, too, so he couldn't put his reaction down to shock at hearing the vulgarity spoken out loud. Although, if he was truthful with himself, shock was definitely part of what he was feeling. It wasn't so much what she'd said, though, as it was the way she'd said it. The emphasis she'd used. *She* was going to fuck *him*.

He was accustomed to it being the other way around. Rodeo groupie, beauty queen or society debutante— they were all content to stand back and let him take the lead. He did the picking and the choosing. He was in charge. His whims and desires dictated the when, the where, and the how. That was the natural order of things and that's the way he liked it.

Although, now that he'd had a minute to think about it, it might be kind of interesting to be the one being done, as it were, instead of the one doing.

Some of Jo Beth's pleasure at having rendered him speechless dissolved as a sly, cocky smile began playing around the edges of his lips again.

"What?" she grumbled, clearly disgruntled at such a short-lived victory.

"Just when were you thinking of doing this…um…" Funny, he found he couldn't say the word as easily as she could. At least, not under the present circumstan-ces. "…of doing it?" he finished lamely.

"It?" Jo Beth arched a derisive eyebrow. "You mean fucking you?"

He scowled. "What kind of language is that for a lady to use?"

"Lady?" Jo Beth gave a spurt of surprised laughter. "Just what century do you live in, cowboy?"

"We're at a wedding," he said reprovingly. "There are children and grandmas present."

Jo Beth made a show of turning her head to take in the dancing couples sharing the floor with them. "None within earshot."

"That's not the point," he insisted, knowing he must sound fairly ridiculous. After all, they'd practically been doing the ol' bump and grind on the dance floor a few minutes ago. But his dear departed mama had raised him to be a gentleman, and a gentleman—or a lady, for that matter—didn't use bad language where children or lit-tle old ladies might overhear. "The point is—"

"The point is, you're a prude," Jo Beth crowed softly, an expression of unholy glee lighting her eyes at find-ing this chink in his facade. "The hotshot stud bull rider is a prude."

It should have turned her off, just like his in-your-face cockiness. The last thing she needed in her life was a judgmental male. Not that he'd be in her life long enough for it to matter, but still, prudery wasn't usually high on her list of the traits she looked for in a sexual partner. And, yet, for some inexplicable and probably highly perverted reason, she found his unexpected streak of modesty...well, hell, *adorable* was the only word she could think of. It was surprising—and surprisingly appealing—in a man who exuded such swaggering sexual confidence. It gave him a vulnerability that made her all the more eager to get him someplace where she could strip him down to his skin and do all the things she'd been fantasizing about doing for the last interminable week. It would add an extra little kick to the proceedings if there were the possibility she might actually manage to shock his socks off while simultaneously screwing his brains out. Maybe she could even make him blush.

"You packing?" she asked, gazing up at him with a look in her eyes that made him instantly suspicious.

"Packing what?"

"Condoms." Under the cover of his tuxedo jacket, she slid her hand from his waist to the back pocket of his trousers and squeezed. "I'll bet you've got a couple in your wallet, right?"

"Yeah." He didn't blush, but he did make a quick scan of the crowd to make sure no one had seen her grope his ass. "So?" he said, with all the wariness of a man who had reached out to pet a house cat and found himself stroking a tiger instead.

His sudden caution pleased her no end. It made up, in no small part, for the incident at the water tank, when he had had the advantage and she had been the one struggling not to show her embarrassment.

"So, I'm going to dance two more dances after this

one," she said, as the fiddler teased the last notes of the song out of his instrument. "And then I'm going to take a stroll down to the corral by the barn to look at Tom's new prize-winning bull. There's a tack room in the northeast corner of the barn, tucked behind the last stall on the right." She leaned into him, lightly touching her breasts to his chest. "It has a door. And a lock," she whispered enticingly, her lips within a kiss of his. "If it won't offend your delicate sensibilities, you can meet me there and we'll play a few of the games I was fantasizing about while you watched me in the water tank yesterday."

The bolt of lust that shot through him at her words burned away all thoughts of propriety and what was or was not appropriate behavior at a wedding. His eyes lit up with pure sexual greed. "Why not all of them?"

"Because there's not enough time. The maid of honor is expected to be present for the cake cutting and the bouquet toss. So's the best man." Just before she drew away, she let her fingertips drift in and downward to brush briefly, lightly, over the fly of his pants. He was as hard as a branding iron under the tailored gabardine fabric. "I'll wait ten minutes. That should be long enough for you to dance a third dance and find your way to the tack room. If you don't show up by then, I'll lock the door and play by myself."

BALANCED ON THE KNIFE'S EDGE of raging lust and the imminent threat of acute embarrassment, the next ten minutes of the wedding reception were the longest of

Clay's life. He danced with the bride and then with the bride's mother while simultaneously thanking providence for tightie-whities and the concealing cut of a classic tuxedo, all the while trying to keep Jo Beth within his line of sight. He watched her out of the corner of his eye as she danced first with Rooster and then with Hector Menendez, his expression much like that of a man watching an exotic animal that had strolled into his backyard—fascinated by its appearance but very aware that it might be more dangerous than it looked.

Jo Beth Jensen certainly fascinated him. And she was certainly more dangerous than she looked in her flimsy bridesmaid's dress. The trouble was, he didn't quite know how or why or in what way that danger might manifest itself. Given the state of his libido at the moment, he didn't much care. For now, it was enough to know that he wanted her. He'd worry about the possible consequences of actually having her later.

Still, he couldn't help but puzzle over it as he danced a third dance, as ordered, and surreptitiously watched her stroll away from the shelter of the white canvas party tent and wander off in the general direction of the barn.

Seen through a connoisseur's critical eye, she wasn't more than passably pretty to look at, even all decked out in her wedding finery. Her face was pleasant but unremarkable, really, except for the intelligence and determination gleaming in her eyes, and the arrogant set of what could otherwise be termed a delicate little chin. He knew for a fact that she did, indeed, have a nice little body and a truly fantastic ass—he'd give her that—but there certainly weren't any beauty-queen curves hiding under the silky material of her bridesmaid's dress. She didn't have a flashy wide-as-the-Texas-prairie smile, either, or big blue eyes with fluttering lashes, and even done up with shiny peach-colored ribbons and tiny white flowers, her hair was still just plain brown. And she sure as hell didn't have what anyone would call an accommodating personality.

So how had she managed to get him hotter, faster, than any woman he'd ever met before?

He was a pretty jaded character, after all, a man who'd sampled just about everything there was to sample, sexually speaking, before the age of twenty-five. Life for a prize-winning rodeo cowboy was a sensual smorgasbord with women laid end to end from one rodeo arena to the next. He didn't have to do much more than crook his finger—and sometimes not even that— to have some curvaceous little buckle bunny ready, willing, and eager to roll over onto her back for him.

He got the distinct feeling Miz Jo Beth Jensen didn't roll over for any man. Hell, she'd probably shoot one who dared to crook his finger at her.

And maybe it was as simple as that. Maybe it was the challenge she offered that lured him so irresistibly and made him salivate like a hound at suppertime when he so much as looked at her. He was a champion bull rider, a man who made his living by pitting himself against creatures that wanted nothing more than to stomp the shit out of him. He *thrived* on challenge, which was something that had been sorely missing from his life lately, and would continue to be missing until he was back on the circuit doing what he'd been born to do.

Looked at from that perspective, it was really no wonder at all that he'd zeroed in on a woman who could give him a real run for his money. It was pure instinct, is what it was, and nothing to be wondered at or puzzled over. Besides which, he had something to prove to hoity-toity Miz Jo Beth Jensen.

He was *not* a goddamned prude!

JO BETH SAUNTERED SLOWLY, carefully, with apparent aimlessness, down the hard-packed, sun-baked path to the barn, both to avoid stirring up the fine powdery dust that would settle on the delicate straps of her heels, and to forestall drawing any undue attention to herself. She didn't want anyone to be able to say later that they had seen her hurrying anywhere, and begin to wonder where she was heading in such an all-fired rush. No sense giving the good folks of Bowie, Texas, anything solid to get their teeth into. She was risking enough already. Probably too much, if you came right down to it. Lord knew what a field day the gossips would have if they had any idea what she was up to! She would be the subject of gleefully appalled tongue-wagging for months if anyone found out she'd disappeared from her best friend's wedding to indulge in a quick bout of slap-and-tickle with the best man. And that man a *cowboy,* for God's sake! A breed she'd publicly sworn off years ago.

She was just the tiniest bit appalled at herself, when

you came right down to it. Not enough to call a halt to the proceedings—she wouldn't give him the satisfaction or deny herself the pleasure—but enough so that she was *almost* hoping he wouldn't show.

In the first place, sex in a barn wasn't all it was cracked up to be. Contrary to popular belief, hay did not make a comfortable bed, even when covered by the ubiquitous plaid blanket seen in all the movies. It was scratchy and dusty, and tended to poke through the blanket to stab the unwary in delicate parts of the anatomy at the most inopportune times. Still, when it was all the bed one had, one made do, and, if one were sufficiently turned on, one barely even noticed how uncomfortable it was. And she was more than sufficiently turned on, and had been since she first clapped eyes on the gorgeous Mr. Clay Madison.

In the second place was the time factor. She figured she had thirty minutes, max, before she was missed. And thirty minutes wasn't enough time to do even half of the deliciously wicked things she'd imagined doing with her fantasy cowboy. It was, however, enough time to do what needed to be done to ease the tension humming crazily through her body.

In the third place, well, there was her heretofore cast-in-iron cardinal rule about not sleeping with cowboys. *That* should have mattered most of all but, strangely enough, it didn't.

Like Scarlett O'Hara, she'd worry about the consequences of her actions tomorrow. Right now, she had an urgent need to scratch an itch that had been driving her crazy for far too long.

Despite her urgency, she stopped by the corral for a moment to admire Tom Steele's new prize-winning Charolais bull—just in case anyone was watching—before slipping into the barn. It was cool and quiet and shadowed inside, with golden dust motes dancing in the bright fingers of sunlight shining in through the shutters in the loft that had been cracked open to provide ventilation and a way for the heat to escape.

"Hello?" she called, and then stood still for a moment, her hand resting on the edge of the door, listening for signs the barn was occupied by more than just livestock. "Hello?"

Hearing nothing but the gentle snuffling of a drowsy horse and the soft chirping of barn swallows nesting in the rafters, she pushed the door closed and headed down the center aisle, between the horse stalls, to the tack room.

Her heels made delicate little clacking noises against the brushed cement floor as she traversed the length of the barn. Her dress swished softly against her calves. Her heart beat wildly in her chest. Her breath sloughed in and out of her lungs, too fast, too heavily, as if she had been running a long way. She stopped for a moment, her palm pressed flat against her chest, and took a few deep controlled breaths in an effort to calm herself down. It was no use. Her breathing—and her heartbeat—continued to race with libidinous excitement.

CLAY TOOK A MORE circuitous route to the barn in an effort to throw anyone who might be watching off the scent. After indicating a need to use the facilities, he headed toward the bunkhouse, then circled around behind it and approached the barn from the far side, out of the line of sight of the guests gathered under the party tent in front of the main house.

He pushed the barn door open with the same stealth Jo Beth had used ten minutes previously, pausing just inside the entrance to let his eyes adjust to the dimness and assure himself there was no one around. A horse nickered as he passed its stall but he spared it no more than a glance as he hurried down the center aisle toward the tack room. His boot heels rang against the cement floor. His suit coat flapped against his hips. His breathing was ragged and quick. He could feel his heart pounding against the wall of his chest and his cock throbbing against the fly of his pants. But none of that stopped him. It didn't even slow his pace.

He rapped once, sharply, impatiently, on the tack room door, and then let himself in before the sound died away.

She was standing, still as a statue, on the opposite side of the small, cluttered room in front of a small, shuttered window. The filtered sunlight created a dappled golden nimbus around her, rimming the edges of her fluttery dress, highlighting the tiny white flowers that adorned her coiffure and the fine wispy strands of hair that escaped her braid, making her look delicate and ethereal. There was a thick pile of quilted stable blankets at her feet, neatly spread out, one atop the other, to create a cozy bed. The invitation inherent in them was blatant and earthy. Clay looked from her face to the blankets and back again.

Their eyes locked.

Held.

"Bolt the door," she said, her voice breathy with excitement.

Without shifting his gaze from hers, Clay fumbled behind him and slid the simple bolt lock home. It made a sharp metallic noise like a rifle being cocked. The noise echoed faintly through the room, sending ripples of sound skittering along their nerve endings. Several more seconds passed in utter silence as they stood stock-still with the width of the room between them, she at the window, he at the door, eating each other up with their eyes.

There was no movement except for the rapid beating of two hearts. No sound except for the labored breath rasping in and out of two pairs of lungs. It was as if they were each waiting for the other to make the next move, to take charge, to commit them both to a course of action that could change everything. Excitement and heat shimmered in the air between them. The sense of anticipation was as ripe and heady as the scent of summer peaches on a hot day.

Jo Beth turned and offered her back. "Unzip me," she ordered, tilting her head forward and reaching around to pull her beribboned braid out of the way.

Clay crossed the room in three long strides and reached out, clasping the tiny tongue of the zipper between his big fingers to pull it down. Her exposed nape was pale and delicate, as vulnerable as a child's above the fabric of her bridesmaid's dress. He could see, close up this time, the fragile bumps of her spine as he slowly lowered the zipper. He leaned down and pressed a kiss between her shoulder blades, just above the ivory satin strap of her bra, then cupped her shoulders, holding her still as he nuzzled his way up her back, to her nape, to the side of her neck.

"Beautiful," he murmured, his lips against her skin.

Jo Beth shivered in response. She arched her neck, letting her body melt back into his for just an instant before she tensed and took a half step away from him. "We haven't got time for any romantic nonsense," she said, as she turned to face him.

His hands remained on her shoulders. "Romantic nonsense?"

"All the tender little touches and sweet talk. We haven't got time for that."

He smiled down into her eyes. "We'll make time," he said, bending his head as if to nuzzle her neck again.

"No." She put a hand on his chest, stopping him. "There's no time. And even if there was—" she shook her head slightly "—I don't need to be wooed, Clay. I know exactly why I'm here and what I want, and I don't need it fancied up and camouflaged with sweet little kisses and pretty lies."

"Most women like it fancied up a bit."

"I'm not most women. I like things to be what they are. And what's between us is sex. Plain and simple. Down and dirty. There's no need to cloud the issue with a bunch of hearts-and-flowers nonsense. We're both here to get laid." She shrugged, her shoulders moving uneasily beneath his caressing hands. "Simple as that."

"So let's just get right to it, is that it?"

"Yes, that's it." Deliberately, her gaze holding his, she slid her hand down the front of his body, cupped her palm over the bulge straining against his fly, and rubbed her thumb over and round the bulging head of his penis. "Any objections?"

Whatever objections he might have had dissolved in a surge of lust so strong, it almost knocked him to his knees. He tightened his grip on her shoulders, dragging her to him, and ran his hands down her back to her butt. He pulled her in, tight against his hips, and ground his pelvis into hers. He took her mouth in a bruising kiss, forcing her head back beneath his, using his lips and teeth and tongue in a way that was blazingly, unabashedly carnal.

She felt devoured. Desired. Deliciously overpowered. Just exactly the way she'd imagined feeling in all her fantasies of him. She sank into it, into *him*, with a murmur of delight. Her mouth was as greedy and voracious as his, her hands busily kneading his chest in a mindless effort to find bare skin. And then she felt his hand scrabbling at the silky material of her dress, inching it up along the back of her thigh, bunching the delicate fabric in his fist.

She tore her mouth away from his. "Wait," she panted. "Wait." She pushed against his chest. It was like pushing against solid granite. "Damn it, Clay. Wait a minute."

He raised his head but didn't let her go. She could feel his breath, hot and rasping against her cheek.

"I thought you wanted it down and dirty."

"I did. I do." Her voice quavered with the effort it took to control her own breathing. "Just let me get my dress off first."

"Screw the dress." His fingers touched the bare skin of her thigh, cupped it, slid upward. "We can work around it."

"No." She grabbed at his hand, as much to stop herself from giving in as to restrain him from going any further. "I can't go back to the reception with my dress all wrinkled. Or torn. Let me take it off."

He dropped his arms and stepped back. "All right." He ran a hand through his hair, giving himself time to take a deep, shaky breath before he could continue. "Take it off."

5

JO BETH TOOK TWO STEPS back from him and, her gaze fastened on his face, reached up and pushed the filmy half sleeves of her dress off her shoulders. She let them fall to the crook of her elbows, let the bodice of the dress slide downward to reveal a hint of cleavage before coyly catching it against her breasts with the flat of her hand. She hadn't intended to do it that way, to drag it out, hadn't intended to make a striptease of it. She had intended, in fact, to dispense with the dress in her usual quick and efficient manner and get on with the business at hand. After all, he'd already seen her bare-assed naked, so it wasn't as if she had anything new to show him.

But there was something in his expression as he watched her remove the dress, something intent and focused and intensely male, something that made her feel intensely female in return. It wasn't just the lust in his eyes—she'd had men look at her with lust before, she *expected* lust in a situation like this—it was the fascination she saw there, the anticipation, the utter raptness of his gaze as he watched the dress slide down. More, it was the blatant, unapologetic sexual greed he made no effort to hide or disguise, as if he wanted to devour her in one big, greedy gulp. It made her feel powerfully, erotically female, and was more arousing than anything she had ever felt before.

She liked it.

A lot.

She wanted more.

She let the dress slide another teasing few inches lower, revealing the curve of her breasts in her strapless ivory satin-and-lace bra. Objectively, she knew how she looked. Her small breasts were plumped up, swelling a bit above the built-in push-up pads in the bra. Her skin was as pale as milk, kept that way through judicious use of sunscreen. She had a smattering of freckles across the tops of her breasts and a tiny mole nestled in her cleavage. Nice enough, but nothing spectacular. Nothing like she knew he was used to. Nothing, really, to rivet his or any man's attention.

And, yet, he was looking at her as if she were built like a Victoria's Secret lingerie model, and he was a man who'd never seen a naked woman before.

With his gaze riveted on her cleavage, he licked his lower lip as if anticipating her taste and the way she would feel in his mouth.

Something tightened deep inside of her, a shaft of longing and lust that was almost painful in its intensity. She lowered the dress another few inches, slowly, catching it in both hands as it slid past the inward curve of her waist, watching his face all the while.

His gaze followed the downward slide of the dress,

his eyes darkening, the pupils expanding to twice their normal size as the peach-colored fabric dipped below her navel.

She held it there, waiting, hoping, yearning for something she couldn't even put a name to.

He forced his gaze upward with visible effort and captured her eyes with his. His expression was that of a man fighting for control. He had to swallow before he could speak. "I thought we didn't have time for romantic nonsense."

"This isn't romantic nonsense." She lowered the dress so that the top edge of her bikini panties showed, and felt a thrill of triumph as his gaze flickered inexorably downward again. "This is to make us both hot."

He shook his head without shifting his gaze. "It's because you like to be in control."

"And that makes you hot, doesn't it?"

"Yeah, it makes me hot." His voice was a hoarse croak but he managed to force his gaze up to hers again. He cocked an eyebrow, casually, as if he wasn't inches away from grabbing her, seconds away from ending the teasing little game she was playing. One corner of his mouth quirked up in the semblance of his usual cocky grin. "How's it working for you?"

She smiled seductively in answer and dropped the dress another few inches, revealing the shadow of dark hair beneath the peekaboo lace of her panties.

Clay sucked in his breath and his hands, hanging loose by his sides, fisted. She could tell he'd come to the end of his rope—and hers. Enough was enough. "Stop playing games and take the dress off, Jo."

She hesitated, wondering how far she could push him, how far she wanted to push him, how far she *dared* push him. He wasn't like the other men she'd bedded. He wasn't a mild-mannered, good-natured banker or a good ol' boy cattle broker, content to let her set the pace and make the rules. He was a cowboy, used to doing things his own way. Though she was loath to admit it, it was one of the things that made him so damned attractive to her.

"Take the dress off. *Now*." His voice was raspy. The look in his eyes was rapacious and predatory, and just a little dangerous. He was a man clearly about to lose what little remained of his control. "Or I swear, I'll take it off for you. And I won't care if it ends up torn and on the floor."

Satisfied by his ragged demand, Jo Beth matter-of-factly lowered the dress to her knees and stepped out of it. Force of habit and inbred practicality had her folding it neatly as she turned to drape it over one of the saddles on the stand behind her to keep it out of harm's way. When she turned back to face him, her arms were already up and behind her, reaching for the hooks on her strapless bra.

"Don't," he ordered.

She paused, her hands still behind her. "Don't what?"

"Don't move. Don't say anything, either," he added, when she opened her mouth to ask why. "Just stand there."

"Why?" she asked, but she let her arms drop back to her sides.

"Not another word," he said, and reached out, pressing his fingertips against her lips, stopping further questions.

She had to fight the urge to kiss them. Or bite them. She wasn't quite sure which. "Why?" she said again, just to keep herself from doing either.

"It's my turn to play games to get us hot. Hotter," he amended. "And you're going to stand there like a good girl and let me play them." He trailed his fingers down over her chin and the delicate line of her throat to the tops of her plumped-up breasts, and then brushed them, back and forth, over the edge of her bra. "Aren't you?"

She nodded. "Yes."

"And you're going to be quiet."

"Yes," she said again, then added. "As long as it suits me."

He gave a strangled bark of laughter. "You don't take orders worth a damn, do you?" His voice was rough, almost savage, but his touch was exquisitely gentle.

"I believe I've already made it clear that I prefer to give them."

"Not this time." He put both hands on her, tracing lazy spirals around her breasts, grazing the bare upper slopes with his calloused fingertips, circling down under the satin-clad lower curves, and up and around again, slowly, drifting closer and closer to her nipples without actually touching them.

She had to fight the urge to grab his hands and *make* him touch her the way she wanted to be touched. The effort caused her muscles to quiver almost imperceptibly, like a barrel racer at the gate or a hound on a scent, sending tremors of anticipation and excitement rippling along her skin.

"You're built real fine," he said musingly, his gaze following the meandering path of his fingers. "Sweet and dainty as a ballerina."

She snorted derisively, or tried to, anyway. The sound was actually more of a whimper. Or maybe a moan.

He slid his hands under her arms, following the band of her bra to the hooks in back. She felt the bra loosen. Instinctively, she tried to tighten her arms to her sides to keep it in place but his arms were in the way. The bra fell to the floor. He stared at her bared breasts for a long appreciative moment. They were as pretty up close as they had been at a distance, small but nicely rounded with tiny raspberry-pink nipples, tumid with arousal that silently begged for his attention. He slid his hands back to the front of her torso and cupped them over her breasts. The slight, sweet swell barely filled his palms.

"Dainty as a ballerina," he repeated decisively, a hint of satisfaction in tone. "I thought so the first time I saw you through Tom Steele's binoculars."

"Binoculars!" The word was barely above a whisper but she got it out. "You were watching me through—"

He pressed his thumbs against her distended nipples.

She sucked in a ragged breath. "—binoculars?" she managed to say as it hissed out again.

"How else was I going to see who was down by the water tank, hmm?"

"What else did you see?"

"You. Doing this." He rotated his thumbs over her nipples, making them stand even more rigidly at attention. "And this." He grasped them between his thumbs and forefingers, pinching them lightly as he'd seen her do, pulling on them until they were jewel hard.

The sound she bit back was *definitely* a moan.

He skimmed his right hand down her belly to trace the edge of her panties. "I couldn't see exactly what you were doing under the water, but I imagine it was something like this." He slipped his hand inside her panties and down between her legs, cupping her.

She clamped her teeth together, determined not to whimper. Or beg.

It turned out she didn't need to.

Clay Madison, cowboy, wild thing, bull rider extraordinaire, was her fantasy come to life. He knew *exactly* what she wanted, *exactly* what she yearned for, and *exactly* how to give it to her. And she didn't have to say a word.

He stroked her clitoris once, very lightly, very slowly, with his index finger, watching her face all the while to gauge her reaction. Evidently, he liked what he saw because he smiled—a slow, sexy, satisfied smile that she would have objected to as smug at any other time—and stroked her again, equally lightly and slowly. And then again…and again…and again, so lightly and slowly and delicately that it was barely a touch at all.

Jo Beth gasped and reached out, grasping his arms to hold herself upright. Her short manicured nails dug into the soft summer-weight wool tuxedo jacket covering his hard biceps. Her eyes closed. She bit down on her lip to stifle the wanting sound that rose in her throat.

"Or maybe it was more like this." He circled the slick, swollen nubbin of sensitized flesh, then grasped it lightly between his thumb and index finger, tugging on it as he had on her nipples.

Jo Beth's entire body jolted in helpless response. Her knees buckled. Her spine arched. Her head fell back. A shuddering sigh escaped her lips.

Yes, he thought with supreme masculine satisfaction, and wrapped an arm around her, catching her up against the hard length of his body. His left hand cradled the back of her head, supporting it as he had when he dipped her on the dance floor. His right continued to work furiously between her legs, two thick blunt-tipped fingers sliding in and out of her now, pressing deep, stroking the exquisitely sensitive upper wall of her vagina, his thumb riding her clitoris. He was determined to bring her to fever pitch, determined to have her explode and melt in his arms like every other woman he'd ever made love to had done.

Another sixty seconds passed in taut, panting silence and then, finally, she uttered a long, low guttural groan of pure unadulterated pleasure and came against his fingers, her wet inner muscles clamping down hard to hold him inside, her fingers white-knuckled as they bit into his biceps.

He bent his head then, capturing the groan with his lips, and immediately set about driving her up again. If one orgasm was good, two was better—and he always aimed to do better. While his fingers continued to gently, expertly ravage the sensitive, swollen passage between her thighs, his mouth ravaged her lips.

She was being invaded above and below, penetrated by his fingers and tongue, caressed into trembling, intemperate insensibility by a man who knew precisely how sex should be done—and who did it with single-minded intensity and admirable attention to nuance and detail.

She came twice more in as many minutes. Small, sharp forceful explosions of sensation that were almost painful in their intensity. She strained against him, trying to get closer and get away at the same time. Her thighs were clamped tight against his hand as if to thwart his invasion while holding him close. Her lips were open and avid under his, inviting him in. Her tongue dueled furiously with his as if to keep him away.

It was too much and not enough, and she wanted more. She wanted it all. She wanted everything she had been fantasizing about for the past interminable week. And she wanted it now. She released her death grip on his biceps and slid her hands up over his shoulders and nape, grasping handfuls of dark silky hair to pull his head up.

"Now," she panted into the scant heated space between their lips. "I want it now."

"Not yet." The words were an automatic assertion of male prerogative, an instinctive reaction to her blatant attempt to dominate the encounter.

Jo Beth's reaction was equally instinctive. She yanked his hair. *"Now,"* she demanded.

Clay reached up and grasped her wrists. "I said—" he enunciated each word very clearly "—not yet."

He pulled her hands down and behind her, anchoring them at the small of her back, holding her immobile, making her feel, strangely enough, both protected and threatened by his rampant unrepentant masculinity.

Jo Beth fought the small traitorous thrill that zinged through her sensitized body, valiantly resisting the urge to melt into him in abject and utter surrender. She stiffened her spine instead, arching away from him, and glared up into his face. "If we're not going to have sex, then let me go."

He grinned. It was the same charming, cocksure oh-so-knowing grin he'd bestowed on her when she was sitting naked in the water tank, the one that whispered of sin and sex and rollicking good times between the sheets.

"Oh, we're going to have sex all right," he assured her. "Just not yet. You're not quite ready yet."

"I'm ready, damn it!"

"Then *I'm* not ready. And I'm the one in charge at the moment." He placed both of her hands in one of his and with the other, reached up to capture her chin. She could smell the musky scent of her arousal on his fingers. She dipped her head, quick as a striking snake, and tried to bite him.

"Bitch," he said, but the word was a caress and he was still grinning that wicked cowboy grin of his.

Aroused, infuriated, inflamed, she lunged forward, aiming to sink her teeth into his shoulder.

He wrapped his hand around her braid and pulled her head back, then bent his own and touched his lips to the underside of her chin.

"You need to learn how to slow it down a little and savor the experience," he said mildly, as if she weren't standing taut and trembling in his arms wearing nothing but her panties and a pair of high-heeled sandals, as if he weren't pressing a gigantic, pulsing hard-on against the softness of her belly, as if he hadn't just finished manipulating her into multiple orgasms that had left her body silently screaming for more. His lips skimmed leisurely down the long, arched line of her throat. Nuzzled her collarbone. Kissed her shoulder. "It's better when you take it slow."

Jo Beth's breath quickened exponentially until she was nearly gasping for air, and she could feel the rapid beating of her heart between her legs in a steady rhythmic pounding that had her fighting the urge to squirm against him.

"We haven't got time to take it slow," she said with admirable calm, despite her heavy breathing and the pounding of her blood. "We have to get back to the reception before people start to miss us."

His lips continued to descend by tiny, delicious increments down her upper chest. "Why?"

"Why?" she echoed faintly, distracted by the warmth of his mouth on her skin. He'd reached the first gentle curve of her breast and was heading inexorably toward her peaked and eager nipple. Oh, God, she wanted his mouth on her nipple! "What do you mean, why?"

"I mean why do you care whether people miss us or not?"

"I care because I live here. And because I don't like to be gossiped about, that's why. Because I don't want everyone knowing that I—" she gasped as he flicked her nipple with his tongue "—that I slipped out to the barn for a quickie at my best friend's wedding. Which they wouldn't if you'd get on with it and stop trying to impress me with what a great lover you are."

Clay sighed heavily and lifted his head. So much for his efforts to seduce and charm her. "All right. You win." He let go of her hair and hands, and straightened. "How do you want it?"

She blinked at his sudden capitulation. "How do I want it?"

"On your back on the blankets? Up against the wall?" He unhooked his black satin cummerbund as he spoke and stuffed it into the pocket of his tuxedo jacket. "Bent over the saddle stand?" He flicked open the button at the waist of his pants. "You're the boss." He lowered the zipper on his fly. "How do you want it?"

"I—" Her glance flickered down to the open V of his pants where a gratifyingly large erection was outlined behind a pair of snug white cotton briefs. Her attention momentarily arrested by the sight, she reached out to touch him.

He was just pissed enough, just disgruntled enough, to deny her what she wanted, even though it meant denying himself, as well. *Talk about cutting your nose— or other parts—off to spite your face,* he thought, as he grabbed her wrist, halting her in midmotion.

"No time for that," he said brusquely. "Just tell me how you want it so we can get this over with and get back to the reception."

Any other woman of his acquaintance would have slapped him or burst into tears or otherwise expressed her displeasure at his crudity and his dismissive tone of voice. But not Miz Jo Beth Jensen. Not the no-nonsense, cool-as-a-cucumber boss lady of the Diamond J ranch. Instead, she stood there, stock-still, her wrist in his hand, actually considering his question.

He could see her thinking about it, could follow her thought process as her gaze darted from the pile of blankets on the floor, to the rough wooden plank wall, to the padded saddle stand. The blankets would be comfortable enough but she'd probably get her hair all messed up and crush all the tiny flowers decorating her fancy French braid. The rough-hewn plank wall might leave splinters in her backside. The saddle stand—

He didn't let her follow the thought to its logical conclusion. Instead, he made the decision for her, just seconds before she could make it for herself. Using the wrist he still held for leverage, he whirled her around in a move that approximated a twirl on the dance floor, put his hand on the back of her neck and pushed her head down, bending her over the padded leather saddle stand before she could so much as whisper a word of protest.

"Don't move," he said, and yanked her panties down to her knees.

Jo Beth had no intention of moving, not when her fantasy was so close to finally being fulfilled. She spread her bare arms out along the padded surface of the saddle rack and arched her back, waiting for the first delicious thrust of his cock. She heard the rustle of foil as he ripped open the condom package, heard the whisper of his trousers as they slid down his legs, felt his big hands cup her hips, and then…nothing.

She hung there for a few seconds more, bent over the saddle rack, her bare bottom thrust up at him, all the small delicate muscles in her body quivering with anticipation and need and lust, desperate to be penetrated, to be taken, to be ridden, damn it! And he was just standing there, his hands on her naked butt, squeezing and stroking it as if he had all day to get the job done. Not that what he was doing didn't feel good. It felt wonderful, in fact, but it wasn't what she wanted…needed…had to have.

Frustrated, irritated, flushed with arousal and desire too long denied, she looked back over her shoulder. "Well?" she demanded, the snap of command in her voice.

"You have a great ass," he said, and slid his palms, fingers spread wide, down over the swelling curve of each buttock. "A world class ass." His extended thumbs touched the moist, pouting folds of her exposed labia.

Jo Beth jerked in reaction.

"Easy," he murmured. "Easy now." He separated the folds, opening her swollen vaginal passage, and gently stroked the edges of her feminine opening.

Jo Beth groaned and dropped her forehead onto the padded leather. "God, you're good at this," she moaned, unable to stop herself from saying it. It was the truth, after all. And it was no surprise. She'd known he would be.

She felt the head of his penis, then, finally, pressing against the vulnerable entrance to her body, felt him enter her that first excruciatingly sensitive inch, felt him withdraw slowly, and then thrust again, a little deeper. And then again, deeper still.

But still not nearly as deep as she wanted him to go.

"You're so huge," she said breathlessly, hoping a little feminine flattery would hurry him along and get her what she wanted. That it was the absolute truth added veracity to the hoarsely whispered words.

"And you're so hot. And wet. And tight," he said, punctuating each word with an increasingly deeper thrust until, at last, *finally,* he was seated to the hilt, completely engulfed in her wetness and heat, completely filling her.

Jo Beth dug her fingers into the padded leather support beneath her cheek and told herself to breathe. Just breathe.

He shifted his hands to her hips, pulling her back against him, holding himself deep inside her, feeling her incredible heat and the tight clasp of her aroused body all along the pulsing length of his penis. It was a staggering, mind-blowing, toe-curling sensation, and one he had obviously too long denied himself judging by his reaction to what was, at base, an experience he'd had countless times before with countless other women. It *couldn't* really be as good as it felt. It was just that it had been too long since the last time. Prolonged abstinence had more to do with his overblown reaction than Jo Beth Jensen's admittedly fantastic ass and glove-tight pussy. Still, his fingers clamped down on her creamy white butt, pulling her closer, holding her tighter, savoring the moment....

"Please," she said, her voice a ragged whisper of need. "Please."

He began thrusting, slowly at first, and then with increasing speed and strength, giving her his full length on each down stroke, nearly withdrawing completely each time he pulled away. His movements were measured and deliberate, plunging deep into her feminine core, withdrawing slowly, plunging again, until she was nearly mad with passion and lust and the need to come.

She pushed against him, her back arched, her legs spread as wide as the panties around her knees would allow, answering each thrust with one of her own, every sinew stretched tight as she reached for the final crest. She rolled her forehead against the saddle stand, breathing hard, blood pounding, her fingers leaving impressions in the supple leather, her whole body straining for the ultimate release.

Oh, yes, *this* is what she wanted, *this* is what she'd been fantasizing about, *this* man inside of her, filling her to bursting, making her writhe and burn.

"Yes," she said in time to his thrusts, the word both an affirmation of pleasure and a demand for more. "Yes. Yes. Yes!"

He picked up the pace, his hips pistoning wildly now, slamming into her. He held her bracketed between his hands, his fingers curved around the voluptuous swell of her hips, holding her steady as he rammed into her. He could feel his heart beating against the wall of his chest, could feel his breath sloughing in and out of his lungs, could feel his cock high and hard and nearly ready to burst.

"Come on, Jo Beth," he coaxed, his voice ragged with the effort of holding back. "Let it go, baby. Let me have it." He reached under her body, stroking her clitoris for added stimulation. "Give it to me. Now."

"Oh, yes. Yes," she moaned as his expert touch pushed her over the precipice into the abyss of pure physical sensation. Her whole body clenched as the tension peaked unbearably, exquisitely, endlessly.

Clay thrust twice more, holding her at the pinnacle, while his own body exploded in a tumultuous climax that curled his toes inside his cowboy boots and nearly made his eyes roll back in his head. He wouldn't have been surprised to feel steam coming out of his ears.

"Oh, yes, Clay. *Yes!*" she screamed softly, collapsing across the padded saddle stand as glorious release drained every last ounce of tension out of her body.

Clay followed her down, his body curving over hers, exhausted, replete, his arms sheltering and cradling her, his breath warm and moist against the back of her neck.

They stayed like that for a few moments, resting together as their breathing evened out and their raging heartbeats slowed to normal. And then he turned his head and pressed a tender kiss on the soft skin beneath her ear. "That was incredible."

"We've got to get back to the reception." She shifted restively beneath him without acknowledging the kiss, or his softly whispered words. "Let me up."

Clay nuzzled her neck. "Most women like a little postcoital snuggling," he murmured persuasively. What he meant was, *he* liked a little postcoital snuggling and most women were more than happy to give it to him.

Jo Beth shrugged away his tender kisses, like a mare shrugging off flies. "I thought we'd already established that I'm not most women," she said coolly.

"No, you damn sure as hell aren't," Clay snapped, thoroughly exasperated with her. Without another word, he pushed himself up and away from her with a hard shove against the saddle stand.

6
_____

THEY RETURNED to Cassie and Rooster's wedding reception the same way they'd left it—separately and unnoticed.

Clay entered the Second Chance bunkhouse through the back door, well out of sight of the people gathered under the white party tent, and sauntered casually out the front a few minutes later, where he joined half a dozen of the male wedding guests who'd left the main body of the party to grab a smoke or chew, and partake of something a little stronger than champagne. Clay waved away the tin of Redman tobacco but accepted a nip from the battered silver flask when it was offered to him. He needed a little something to fortify him after what had happened in the barn. And he didn't mean the sex.

The sex had been great. The sex had, in fact, been absolutely fantastic. Far from being a prissy, dried-up stick, Jo Beth Jensen was a juicy, passionate, demanding woman. Emphasis on the demanding. She'd gotten him hotter, harder, faster than any woman had in a good long while. A big part of that was, of course, that it had _been_ a good long while, but he was fair-minded enough to give the devil her due. She was a sexual dynamo, with enough sensual heat to fry a man's brain. That didn't mean, though, that he still wasn't just the slightest bit pissed at her. Okay, he was more than slightly pissed. He was a lot pissed.

She'd used him like a goddamned stud!

Talk about wham-bam-thank-you-ma'am or, in this case, thank-you-sir. And he hadn't even gotten the thank-you. When she'd gotten what *she* wanted, she'd pulled up her lace panties, shimmied into her dress, smoothed a hand over her hair, and beat a hasty retreat without even a kiss goodbye.

"Give me a two minute head start and don't leave the same way you came in," she said before she slipped out the door.

He was left standing in the tack room, his pants unzipped, his crumpled cummerbund hanging out of his jacket pocket, listening to the rapid clickity-clack of her heels on the brushed cement floor of the barn as she hurried away from him.

He wasn't used to that kind of cavalier treatment from a woman. Especially not from a woman he'd just made love to. Women he'd just made love to—starting with Tish Bradley in his sophomore year in high school and continuing right on down to the buckle bunny who'd availed herself of his services in the hospital bed after the run in with ol' Boomer—were normally loath to let him go. Women *he'd* just made love to wanted kissing and cuddling and, usually, another go-round. And he was always more than happy to oblige. To his mind, the kissing and cuddling—both before and after the main event—were part of what made sex so much fun and, not coincidentally, kept the ladies coming back for more.

Obviously, Miz Jo Beth Jensen didn't share the general feminine view as to the desirability of the myriad sexual pleasures to be had outside of the act itself. Or she just wasn't interested in another turn with him. The first possibility was an affront against nature. The second was, frankly, inconceivable. Both were an insult to his skills as a lover.

Clay Madison wasn't a man who took an insult lying down, and he plumb hated to see a woman miss out on the plethora of physical pleasures available to her sex. As he set himself to rights, he began pondering all the ways in which he might rectify the situation to their mutual advantage.

WITH HER FOREARMS casually crossed atop the paddock fence adjoining the barn, Jo Beth made it a point to be found admiring Tom Steele's newly acquired Charolais bull. The massive animal was long-bodied and heavily muscled, and sported moderate-sized horns atop his majestic head. His hide was creamy white with beige mottling on his flanks and belly. His muzzle was an incongruously delicate pink.

"Fine animal," she said as the bull's owner strolled up beside her, "but I still think you should have gone with a Brahman. Crossbred to your Herefords, you'd've still gotten a decent lean-to-fat ratio without sacrificing your reproduction rate."

Tom propped his forearms on the fence next to her

and lifted one booted foot to rest on the bottom rung. "I'm not worried about the reproduction rate with this big boy," he said. "Besides, Brahmans are ornery cusses. Most of 'em would sooner stomp on you as look at you."

Jo Beth arched an eyebrow, slanting him an amused, slightly patronizing glance. "That's your rodeo background talking," she chided. "Brahmans are as docile as lambs if you know how to handle them."

The implication was, of course, that he didn't know how to handle them. She didn't often revert to taking potshots at her ex almost-fiancé these days. She'd gotten past the hurt feelings a long time ago and had come to the realization that they got along much better as friends and neighbors than they ever would have as husband and wife. Besides, when you came right down to it, he *was* only an almost fiancé; he'd never actually asked her to marry him, not in so many words. But he'd been planning to ask her. He knew it and she knew it, and the whole town of Bowie, Texas, knew it. It had been understood by all concerned that he was going to have one final rodeo season, one final fling, and then he was going to come home and settle down with the cowgirl next door.

Instead, he'd come home in the middle of that season with a sexy blonde in tow and married her in Las Vegas during the rodeo finals in December.

It had taken months for Jo Beth to get over the humiliation of being so publicly dumped. But she had and, in the nearly five years since then, she'd become good friends with his wife and had even managed to forgive him for not living up to her—and their neighbors'—matrimonial expectations. Mostly. Sometimes, though, she couldn't help but poke at him a little.

He was, after all, the cowboy who had, well…not broken her heart, exactly, but he'd sure as hell battered her pride. It wasn't a thing a woman forgot. So, sometimes, especially when she was feeling a little mean to begin with, she took a verbal swipe at him.

And she was feeling more than a little mean at the moment, despite the fact that she'd just experienced the best orgasm of her life. Or, hell, maybe she was feeling mean *because* she had just experienced the best orgasm of her life and knew it wasn't an experience that had a snowball's chance in hell of ever being repeated.

Not if she was smart, anyway, because she'd been right in her initial assessment of the consequences of allowing herself to indulge in the reality of Clay Madison. He wasn't going to be easy to forget and, after just one memorable, mind-blowing quickie, both the cattle broker in Dallas and good ol' Todd in the next county were going to suffer by comparison. Another tumble with Clay Madison could put her off other men altogether, leaving her with nothing but fantasies to ease her frustrations. Just the mere thought of it made her feel spiteful.

"That big boy isn't going to endure a Texas summer as well as my Brahmans," she said, her tone just short of snide. "And his size is going to make calving difficult for your Hereford cows."

"I've got plenty of cowboys to pull calves, if need be."

"Unlike me, you mean?"

"I didn't say that," Tom said mildly, refusing to take offense. "And you know anytime you need help with calving, or anything else, all you have to do is ask."

She batted her lashes at him. "And the big strong cowboy will come to my rescue?" The words and the gesture were teasing; her tone was not.

"Jesus, Jo." Tom straightened away from the fence to stare down at her, baffled by her attack. He'd've sworn he hadn't done anything to set her off. Unless being neighborly had become a crime when he wasn't looking. "What put the burr under your saddle this time?"

"Nothing." She shook her head at him. "Forget it. I'm sorry. I'm being bitchy." She passed a hand over her forehead to hide her eyes from his searching gaze. "I guess I'm still feeling the effects of last night's bachelorette party."

"Headache?" he said, instantly sympathetic. His wife Roxy had come home from the bachelorette party with a doozy of a headache that had taken three extra-strength aspirin and an afternoon nap with an ice pack on her head to eradicate. And she'd still been just a tiny bit wobbly on her pins when it was time to leave for the church.

Jo Beth lifted one shoulder in a halfhearted shrug, not wanting to tell an outright lie. One of her sacred duties as maid of honor was *not* to drink so much at the bachelorette party that she had a hangover at the wedding. And she hadn't, but, hey, it was as good an excuse as any for her bad mood. "Humph," she mumbled, hoping that would suffice.

"Well, hell, honey, you should know better than to stand bare-headed in the sun when you're hung over." Tom proffered his arm, elbow bent, like the born-and-bred Texas gentleman he was. "Come on back to the party tent and we'll get Roxy to round you up a couple of aspirin before the cake-cutting ceremony."

ONCE THE CAKE WAS CUT, the reception began to wind down rapidly. Rooster and Cassie had a plane to catch—they were headed to San Francisco for their honeymoon—and most of the party guests were ranchers and working folks who had to get up early to do chores and attend to business. By eleven o'clock, the band had packed up and gone, and the red taillights of various pickups and four-wheel-drive SUVs flickered in the distance as the last guests headed down the long graveled driveway toward the road and home.

Jo Beth had morning chores, too, of course, and she considered using them as an excuse to leave when the other guests did, but, as the maid of honor, another of her duties was to take charge of the wedding dress Cassie had left behind when she'd changed into her going-away outfit, and to round up and secure the wedding gifts brought to the reception.

Clay didn't have any chores he could claim, and wouldn't have if he did. As best man and a guest at the Second Chance he was obliged by country tradition and good manners to stick around and help his hosts clean up.

"Oh, Lord, let's leave the rest of this mess for the morning," Roxy said, when they had made enough progress so that opossums, raccoons and other night critters wouldn't be tempted by what was left. "Grab that last stack of plates there, will you, Clay sugar, and let's all go in the kitchen and put our feet up. I don't know about y'all, but I need a nice hot cup of coffee and a good gossip to settle all that champagne and cake."

"Coffee?" Clay gave an exaggerated shudder as he followed his hostess up the porch steps and through the back door into the heart of the house. "At this hour?"

"I'm sure Tom could be convinced to crack open a bottle of sippin' whiskey, if you'd rather have that. Me, I want coffee. I've about had my quota of alcohol for the entire year in these last few days. How 'bout you, Jo Beth?" Roxy asked as Jo Beth came clattering down the back stairs into the kitchen.

Jo Beth peered around the edge of the bulky white dress box she held awkwardly in both arms. "How 'bout me, what?"

"Coffee or whiskey as a nightcap?"

"Neither, thanks. It's been a long day and I really should be getting ho—" The scent of the rich French-roast grounds Roxy was spooning into a paper filter reached out across the room to tantalize her. "Okay, you hooked me. One cup," Jo Beth said, and eased the dress box to the floor to lean it against the kitchen counter. The oversize shopping bag slung over her shoulder swung forward with the movement, threatening to spill Cassie's white satin shoes and various other wedding paraphernalia over the floor.

"Whoa, there." A large tanned hand reached out to

steady it. "Let me help you with that," Clay said, attempting to slide the bag off of her arm.

Jo Beth sidled away from him like a skittish mare, resettling the bag on her shoulder to cover her instinctive retreat. She hadn't seen him when she'd come into the kitchen and his sudden appearance at her side had, quite naturally, startled her. At least, that's what she told herself.

"Thanks. I've got it," she said, and wondered if it would cause undue speculation if she decided against staying for that last cup of coffee, after all.

A quick glance at Clay's face decided her. He flashed her a quick, self-satisfied little smile, an I-know-what's-got-you-on-the-run smirk that instantly put her back up. She let the shopping bag slide down off her shoulder and plopped it on the floor next to the dress box. "Could I maybe get a tiny smidge of that whiskey in my coffee?" she said as she pulled out a chair at the kitchen table and sat down.

"A little hair of the dog that bit you?" Tom said as he turned from the distressed-pine cupboard that served as the Steele's liquor cabinet with a squared-off bottle in his hand. It had a familiar black label. "Clay? You want yours in your coffee, too?"

Clay shook his head. "Straight up." He pulled out the kitchen chair opposite Jo Beth, swung it around, and straddled it. "Coffee'd keep me up all night," he said blandly, although the look in his eyes as he stared across the table at Jo Beth was anything but.

Jerk, she thought, and narrowed her eyes at him, trying to telegraph boredom and aloof indifference.

It would have been easier if he weren't so damned hot. He'd discarded his tuxedo jacket and rolled back the cuffs of his pin-tucked white dress shirt, showing off strong, tanned forearms. His black silk bow tie hung loose around his collar, the ends dangling down the front of his shirt, framing the narrow hair-dusted wedge of chest peeking out from between the shirt buttons he'd also loosened.

During their all-too-brief encounter in the tack room, she hadn't had a chance to touch his bare chest, or even see it. That was a major disappointment and a major fantasy left unfulfilled because, from what little she could see, it was a damned fine chest, heavily muscled, lightly tanned, deliciously hairy.

Clay's knowing smirk widened into a grin.

Jo Beth cut her eyes away from him dismissively and stood up. "Can I help you with anything, Rox?"

Roxy put a heavy white china mug on the table in front of Jo Beth's chair. "You could grab some forks from the drawer there behind you, if you would, sugar."

"Forks?"

"For the cake."

"There's more cake?" Clay said, his face lighting up like a kid's at the mention of dessert. "Devil's food or white cake?"

"Devil's food." Roxy smiled indulgently and placed a large slab of thickly frosted devil's food groom's cake in the middle of the table. "There's only this one piece left." She shrugged a little sheepishly at Jo Beth's incredulous look. "It'd be a shame to waste it."

"We won't waste it," Clay assured her.

"Oh, what the hell," Jo Beth said, and got the forks.

A few moments later, all four of them were sitting around the scarred wooden kitchen table in their rumpled wedding finery, eating devil's food cake from a communal platter.

Jo Beth tried not to watch as Clay lipped chocolate cake off the tines of his fork, tried not to pay any attention to the play of tendons and veins in his bared forearms, tried not to show any interest in the way his throat worked when he swallowed, tried desperately not to let her fascination show.

It wasn't as if he were doing anything deliberately erotic. At least, not that she could tell. He was just sitting there, happy as a ten-year-old boy, eating chocolate cake in the company of friends. It was her own raging libido that infused his every move with raw sensuality and made it necessary for her to avoid intercepting his gaze lest she give herself away.

"So, Jo." Tom licked last bit of frosting off his fork and picked up his whiskey. "You hire any extra hands, yet?"

Jo Beth had to swallow before she could answer. "Not yet," she said, thankful she had something to focus her attention on besides the way Clay Madison looked eating cake. "And I had another one quit on me yesterday."

Tom raised a questioning eyebrow.

"Jimmy Billings decided he could make more money roping steers on the circuit than he could working for me." She mashed a few of the remaining cake crumbs with the tines of her fork. "He probably can, too. He's good enough to pull down some decent prize money."

"So now you're what? Two hands short? Three?"

"Three." She licked the fork clean and placed it, tines pointed down, on the edge of the cake platter. "This time of year it wouldn't normally be a problem because I can usually make do with fewer hands once the spring calving season is over. But I've got those dudes coming in a couple of days." She sighed and took a sip of her whiskey-laced coffee. "I've got a feeling they're going to need a whole lot more handling than my cows."

"Could you use a couple of boys part-time?" Roxy asked. Besides being a working cattle ranch, the Second Chance Ranch was also a group home for delinquent and abandoned boys. "A couple of our older ones—" Roxy always referred to the boys in her care as *ours* "—are turning into good cowhands. I know they'd be interested in picking up a little extra cash. It'd only be part-time, though," she reiterated. "They have summer-school classes."

"Sure, that'd be great. Send them on over and we'll figure out a schedule that'll work with their schooling."

"That still leaves you one hand short," Tom reminded her.

"Yeah, well…" She finished off the last of her coffee. "I'll work something out. I always do."

"I'd be happy to lend a hand," Clay said, surprising himself as much as everyone else.

He'd had no idea he was going to make the offer until he heard it coming out of his mouth. Once he'd said it, though, it sounded like a really good idea. A brilliant idea, in fact.

He'd already come to the conclusion that all he needed was a little time and proximity to convince Jo Beth she was interested in another go-round with him. The only question nagging at him had been how he was going to manage it without looking as if he were trying to manage it and, suddenly, here was the perfect solution. Lending a hand on her ranch would be the perfect way to get close enough to persuade her she wanted another taste of what he had to offer without looking as if he were chasing after her like a hound with his tongue hanging out.

Before Jo Beth could think of a really good reason— one she could share, anyway—why it was a really *bad* idea, Tom seconded the notion.

"I don't know why I didn't think of that myself," he said. "It's the perfect solution to both your problems."

"*Both* our problems?" Jo Beth said. "What do you mean, both our problems?"

"You need a cowhand. Clay needs something to do to keep him from going stir-crazy while he finishes healing up from that last wreck."

"I need an *experienced* cowhand, not a la-di-da rodeo star." Jo Beth cast a disparaging glance at Clay. "No offense intended," she assured him mendaciously.

"None taken," he said, equally untruthful.

"Clay's more than a rodeo star," Tom said indignantly, insulted on Clay's behalf. "He grew up on a cattle ranch up in… Where was it, Clay?"

"Nebraska," Clay said.

"Nebraska. That was it. It's good cattle country up there. Not as good as Texas, of course, but running cattle is running cattle, no matter where you do it."

"But I thought you planned to head on home in a few days," Roxy said, "so you could visit with your family while you heal up."

"Nebraska isn't home. Leastways, not since my folks died." Clay jerked his thumb over his shoulder, aiming in the general direction of the back door. "That rig outside is home. My aunt Lorraine and her husband invited me to park it at their place until I was healed up enough to go back on the circuit." He shrugged. "We aren't real close, though. It wouldn't hurt any feelings or ruffle any feathers if I called and said I wasn't coming. Truth be told, they'd probably be glad not to have to put up with me."

"I need someone for the entire summer," Jo Beth said, ignoring the little spurt of sympathy she felt at his careless words. She knew a lot of professional rodeo cowboys lived in trailers like his. Most of them appeared to prefer it that way but it had always seemed to her to be a lonely rootless way to live. In any case, his living conditions weren't any of her concern. What was her concern was her ranch.

"I'm not interested in hiring a cowhand who'll be heading back to the rodeo as soon as he's healed up," she said. "I need someone who'll stick around for the whole season."

"I'm not going anywhere near a rodeo for at least three months," Clay said. "Doctor's orders."

"You'd have to put in a full day's work. I can't afford to be paying wages to someone who can't pull their weight."

"I don't expect you to pay me any wages at all," Clay said. "My offer's strictly neighborly. Besides, you'd be providing me with a place to park my rig. That's payment enough."

"Oh. Well." It took her a second or two to think of a rejoinder to that. "I'd still expect a full day's work, wages or not. There's no room for slackers on the Diamond J."

"I can do a full day's work," Clay assured her, his tone just the slightest bit testy. No one had ever questioned his work ethic before. "And then some. The only thing I *can't* do right now is ride bulls." His gaze turned deliberately seductive. "I can ride anything else I can get my leg over, though."

"I'm sure you can," she said, her gaze as steely as his was hot. "But your expertise as a rider isn't what I need."

"And what *do* you need?"

Jo Beth ignored the implication in his question. "What I need is someone who can interact with the dudes," she said, hoping that would put him off the idea. "Someone who can make them feel like they're participating without letting them get in the way or get into trouble."

"That doesn't sound too difficult."

"I'd expect you to cater to them," she said, making it up as she went along. "Put up with their whims. Run errands, even, if that's what it takes to keep them happy."

"Like I said—" he shrugged "—that doesn't sound too difficult."

"Not difficult, maybe. But it wouldn't be anything like you're used to."

His lips turned up in a rueful little smile. "Pretty much nothing in my life lately is like what I'm used to."

"And, hell, Jo, think how impressed the dudes would be," Tom said.

"Impressed with what?"

"With Clay, that's what. With having a real live rodeo cowboy in their midst. A four-time bull-riding champion, no less. Your dudes would get a real thrill out of it."

"I don't see why," Jo Beth said dismissively, although she did, all too clearly.

"No, Tom's right," Roxy chimed in loyally. "Rodeo's gotten to be a real popular sport, especially bull riding. It's on ESPN all the time. The dudes would love it." She flashed one of her thousand-watt smiles at Clay. "Especially the women."

"Oh, that's just what I need," Jo Beth countered. "A hip swaggering rhinestone Romeo running around loose on the Diamond J, seducing my female guests. That'd go over *real* big with the husbands."

"I've never worn a rhinestone in my life," Clay objected. "And I've never trifled with a married woman."

Jo Beth raised an eyebrow at that.

"That I know of," Clay amended.

"See there?" Tom said. "He knows how to behave proper."

"I'm sure he knows how," Jo Beth agreed. "The question is, would he?"

"Jo Beth!" Roxy said, scandalized. "There's no call to be hateful."

"I'm sorry. You're right." She looked across the table at Clay. "I apologize. I had no cause to make an assumption like that. No offense," she said, meaning it sincerely this time.

"None taken," he replied, equally sincere.

"Well, now, it's settled then," Tom said, satisfaction evident in his tone. "Clay'll move his rig on over to your place in the morning so he can be on hand to help you wrangle the dudes."

"Jo Beth hasn't said whether she's agreeable to that, yet," Roxy pointed out.

"Jo?" Tom said.

Jo Beth looked across the table at Clay. "Riding herd on a bunch of dudes isn't the kind of work you're used to," she said, giving it one last shot. "It isn't going to be exciting or stimulating or probably even very interesting. You'll likely be bored out of your mind before the week is out."

"No more bored than I'd be hanging around my aunt's place doing nothing all summer except rest up." He stood and extended his hand across the table. "I'm willing to give it a try if you are." He grinned. "Boss?"

Jo Beth had no choice. Not with Tom and Roxy and Clay staring at her, waiting for her answer. Not when it was, as Tom had said, damn it, the perfect solution to both her and Clay's problems. If he were anyone else, she wouldn't hesitate for a minute.

That in itself was reason enough to accept his offer because if she turned him down it was a sure bet everyone in the county would start in to speculating as to why, and getting it all wrong in the process. Or not.

She stood, reaching across the table to put her hand in his. "I'll see you bright and early tomorrow morning." She gave his hand one hard pump and let it go. "The day starts at 5:00 a.m. on the Diamond J."

7

"*SEÑORITA* JO?" Esperanza Diego tapped lightly on the door frame of Jo Beth's open office door. "You have company, *señorita*."

Jo Beth knew who the company was. She'd heard the muted roar of his high-powered pickup as it had pulled into the yard, heard his knock on the front door, heard the low, easy timber of his voice as he conversed in soft sibilant Spanish with her housekeeper, heard his boot heels ring confidently against the polished terra-cotta tiles in the wide front hall as he made his way toward her office across from the kitchen.

She was ready for him. More than ready. She'd been mentally preparing herself for this meeting since the minute she'd opened her eyes that morning. She knew exactly what she was going to say and exactly how she was going to say it. There would be no room for misunderstanding or innuendo, and she would make it absolutely clear that if he were going to work on the Diamond J, there would be no repeat of what had happened in the tack room in Tom Steele's barn. No matter how indiscreetly she may have behaved with a fellow member of the wedding party, the jefe of the Diamond J did not indulge in sexual antics with the hired help. Period. Full stop. End of story.

She was fairly certain that knowledge would cause Clay to rescind his offer to help. She knew, as surely as she knew her own name, that he'd only made the offer because he thought it would get him into her pants again. And if she was wrong, if he really had made the offer out of the goodness of his heart or as an antidote to boredom or some combination of the two, well, at least she'd have made her position clear and there would be no misunderstandings or ambiguities that might come back to haunt her later.

"*Gracias,* Esperanza," she said coolly, without looking up from the spreadsheet on her computer screen. "Ask him to come in, *por favor.*"

"I'm already in," he said.

Jo Beth looked up to see him standing in the doorway beside and just a bit behind her housekeeper. He towered head and shoulders above the diminutive woman, looking dark and dangerous and fatally seductive in snug, faded jeans that hugged his lean hips and a snap-front western shirt that made his shoulders and chest look impossibly broad. His stacked-heel cowboy boots were burnished black leather, hand-stitched and custom-made, adding unnecessary inches to his height. A silver trophy buckle—one of hundreds, she was sure—decorated his hand-tooled leather belt and showcased his lean midsection. The silver conchas running down the sides of his chaps emphasized the length of his lean horseman's legs and subtly accentuated the bulge beneath his fly. He was every inch the cocky, confident rodeo heartthrob, from the dark, silky hair tickling the tops of his ears, to the black cowboy hat he carried, deceptively gentlemanlike, in one hand, to the blunted rowels of the diamond and heart spurs on his boots.

Jo Beth ignored the fluttering sensation in her chest and told herself she wasn't the least bit impressed.

"He is already in," Esperanza parroted, turning her head to smile up at him approvingly.

"So I see," Jo Beth muttered, wondering if he deliberately went out of his way to charm every woman he came in contact with, or if it came so naturally to him he didn't even know he was doing it.

Like Jo Beth, the housekeeper wasn't normally an easy woman to charm but, somehow, someway, he had accomplished that task in the time it took to walk from the front door of the ranch house to the office. Esperanza was all but simpering.

"*Gracias,* Esperanza," Jo Beth said again, tacitly sending the housekeeper on her way.

"*Sí, señorita.*" Esperanza bobbed her head and stepped back. She bumped into Clay.

He turned sideways, pressing his back up against the doorjamb to let her get by, and made a flourishing gesture with the hat in his hand that ceded the right of way to her. She flashed another twinkling smile at him. He returned it instantly and in full measure, giving the housekeeper a look that said, at just that moment, his entire attention was centered squarely and completely on her. That ability to focus so intently on a single person was a big part of his charm, Jo Beth realized, and whether it was learned or innate made no difference in how it affected people.

"You're late," she said pointedly, when he turned that laserlike attention back to her. She stiffened her spine against its softening effect.

"Late?" A ghost of a grin turned up the corners of his mouth. "You mean you were *serious* about starting at five o'clock?"

Jo Beth didn't return his smile. "I'm always serious when it comes to the Diamond J. You'd do well to remember that."

"Yes, ma'am." He touched two fingers to his forehead in a mocking salute. "I'll make a note of it."

Jo Beth stifled a sigh. He wasn't going to make this easy but, then, she really hadn't expected him to. His type never did things the easy way if they could help it. "Come in and close the door, please," she said in her most clipped, most authoritative voice. "If you're actually going to go through with this charade, there are a few things I need to make crystal clear to you first. Privately."

He closed he door. "Sounds serious." He sauntered across the small room, hitched a hip onto the edge of her desk and, placing his forearm on his thigh, leaned in as if ready to listen intently. "Shoot," he said.

Jo Beth tensed, fighting the cowardly urge to get to her feet and put some space between them. "You're crowding me," she said instead. Her voice was cool and rock steady. She was very proud of herself for the way it sounded; it was so completely at odds with the warm, squishy, entirely *idiotic* way her insides were reacting to his nearness. "And I don't like to be crowded." She leveled an icy gaze at him for emphasis. "So back off, cowboy."

Clay straightened away from her without rising from the edge of the desk. "Whatever you say, boss."

"I don't like to be called boss, either," she snapped.

"Is there anything you *do* like?"

So much for there being no room for innuendo, she thought. The man was a master at it. Sexual insinuations came as easily to him as breathing. Or, hell, maybe she was hearing sensual implications that weren't there. She didn't think so, though. He looked way too self-satisfied and full of himself for her to be imagining it.

She stifled another sigh. "Look," she began patiently, determined to stick to the script she had devised in her head. "If you're going to be working here we have to get a few things straight."

"Such as?"

"Such as how there will not be a repeat of what happened at the wedding reception yesterday."

The expression in his dark eyes warmed another lascivious degree or two. "In the tack room, you mean?"

"Yes, in the tack room." She pushed to her feet, unable to sit still another minute with him perched on the edge of her desk, looming over her, all but surrounding her with his heat and raw animal vitality. "I want to be absolutely clear on this. It will not happen again."

"Why not? Didn't you like it?" His smile made it clear that he knew she had.

"That's not the point."

"What is the point, then?"

"The point is, I am the jefe of the Diamond J and as such I don't indulge in intimate relationships with the hired help."

"Well, you know, strictly speaking, I'm not the hired help." He fingered the brim of his hat as he spoke and tilted his head, looking up at her from under his thick fringe of lashes, suddenly the very picture of harmless aw-shucks innocence. "I'm just somebody who's being real neighborly-like and lending a—" his glance flickered downward for a scant, fleeting second "—hand."

Jo Beth had to restrain the urge to shield the crotch of her jeans with her palms. So much for innocence! "This isn't going to work," she said.

"Oh, I think it will." He rose from his perch on the edge of the desk and set his hat, brim side up, on top of her computer monitor. "You just have to adjust your perspective a little bit, is all."

"My perspective?" She stood her ground as he moved toward her, despite the insistent clamoring of every single nerve ending she possessed telling her to turn tail and run. Jo Beth Jensen had never run in her life and she wasn't about to start now. "What's wrong with my perspective?"

"First off, we don't have an intimate relationship. We don't have any kind of relationship at all, when you come right down to it."

"No, we don't," she agreed. "We *don't* have a relationship. That's exactly what I wanted to make clear." She took a small unconscious step back as he continued to advance with that slow hip-rolling cowboy gait of his that oozed sex with every step. "I'm glad you realize that, and that you're willing to acknowledge it. I wasn't sure you would."

"Oh, I realize it. I realized it from the minute you told me what we *do* have."

"*I* told you what we have? When?"

"In the tack room."

"I told you…?" She shook her head, unable to think clearly with him standing so close. And, come to think of it, how had he gotten so close? And how had she ended up with her back pressed flat against the metal file cabinet?

This wasn't how she'd meant this interview to go at all. She'd been determined to stand her ground, to show him who was boss, to show him how unaffected she was by his seductive charm and, yet, here she was, cornered in her own office, as breathless and wet as some brainless hot-to-trot buckle bunny.

She slapped her hand against his chest to hold him off. "What did I tell you we have?" she demanded, striving to maintain some semblance of control.

He put his hand over hers, pressing it flat to his chest. "Don't you remember?"

She could feel the slow, steady beat of his heart beneath the hard curve of his pectoral muscle. It set her palm to tingling and sent heat racing up her arm to sear her brain, making it hard to connect one coherent thought to another. She shook her head again, trying to clear the sensual haze that fogged it.

"You explained that what was between us was sex," he reminded her. "Plain and simple, down and dirty sex, you said. And then you slid your hand down my body—" he matched the words to action, dragging her hand, unresisting, down the front of his body as he spoke "—and showed me exactly what you meant by that."

She could feel his erection under her palm, huge and hard and tempting, pushing against the button-fly front of his jeans, throbbing under her fingers. He released her hand. She didn't move it. She barely even breathed.

"It was good sex," he said, his voice low and dark and wickedly seductive. "It was hot, wild, mind-blowing, toe-curling sex. I want more. How 'bout you, Jo Beth?" He nudged his hips forward, pressing his erection more deeply into the curve of her hand. "Do you want more, too?"

There was only one honest answer to that but she couldn't quite bring herself to say it. She couldn't bring herself to move her hand, either. That was answer enough.

"We could have more." He bracketed her hips in his palms and pulled her firmly to him, so they were pressed tightly together, pelvis to pelvis.

Her hand was trapped between their bodies, her palm filled with his hard, hot penis, her knuckles pressed against her own pubic mound. All the soft, sensitive tissue between her thighs began to tingle.

"I'd be at your service, just like in the tack room," he said. "Only it wouldn't be a quickie. I'd make it last for hours."

"Hours?" she echoed faintly, thinking of all the fantasies she'd had over the last week, fantasies of what she could do to him…what he could do to her…what they could do to each other. The throbbing between her thighs intensified.

"Hours," he promised. "Think about it, Jo Beth. You and me together." He bent his head and nuzzled the hollow of her throat, his lips barely touching her, his breath hot and moist against her skin. "Completely naked." His mouth grazed the side of her neck and trailed upward. "In a bed." He flicked the lobe of her ear with his tongue. "I'm good in a bed." He breathed the words into her ear. "Real good."

Coming from any other man the hotly whispered words would have sounded like sheer macho braggadocio. From him, they were merely a statement of fact— and she could testify to the truth of that statement from her own experience.

He *was* good.

Damned good.

He was, unfortunately, the best she'd ever had.

"I can give you what you want." He shifted her hips from side to side between his hands as he spoke, so that their bodies rubbed together, so that she felt the pressure of her own hand between her legs. "As often as you want it. Any way you want it."

She closed her eyes and sucked in her breath, wondering if she was going to come right then and there, just from the sound of his voice in her ear and feel of him in her hand and the exquisite intermittent, maddening pressure against her pubic bone.

"Anything you want," he whispered hypnotically, like the legendary incubus of Greek myth, promising untold sexual delights to susceptible women. He rotated his hips, just slightly, just enough to make her gasp and catch her breath. "Anything you can imagine."

"Anything?" she murmured, transfixed, her imagination running riot, her blood pounding, her body pulsating with anticipation and rampant intemperate need.

"Anything." His lips grazed hers, barely touching. "And everything," he said, the words a hot promise against her mouth.

And then he let her go and stepped back.

"Or we could do it your way," he said, "and keep it strictly business."

Jo Beth blinked up at him, dazed, confused, wildly aroused, her lashes fluttering like those of a dreamer caught in a deep, drugged sleep.

"Think about it," he said, "and let me know." He plucked his hat from the top of her computer. "I'll be outside getting my rig situated."

IT TOOK JO BETH nearly sixty seconds to tamp down the urge to chase after Clay so she could throttle him with her bare hands. And then another sixty to come to the inescapable conclusion that she didn't really want to throttle him—when she finally got her hands on him it would be to do something far different!—and didn't need to think about whether to accept his offer or not. Well, she did *need* to think about it, she *should* think about it, but damn it, she didn't *want* to think about it!

She wanted him. She wanted her fantasy cowboy and the hours of hot, wild, mind-blowing, toe-curling sex he had offered her. And, at that exact moment, with her body still throbbing and her blood running hot and her nerves screaming with sheer sexual frustration, she couldn't think of one single reason why she shouldn't have what she wanted. Not one.

As long as she went about it discreetly, so there was no chance of anyone ever knowing, what was the harm? As he had pointed out, he wasn't actually an employee. She wasn't paying him a salary. So, in reality, she wasn't violating her rule against getting involved with the hired help. And her other rules, the ones about not getting involved with cowboys and not indulging her sexual appetites close to home, well, she'd already violated both of those by having sex with him yesterday. At this point it was just a matter of degree and, hell, in for a penny, in for a pound, as her mother used to say.

Her mind made up, she plucked her hat off the rack by the door, settled it securely on her head, and calmly, deliberately, headed outside to the yard to lay down the terms of their continued…association.

Clay was standing by the hood of his gleaming black pickup, hipshot, at ease, talking to T-Bone McGuire and two teenaged boys she recognized from the Second Chance Ranch.

The boys, brothers by the look of them, were sandy-haired and gangly, wearing faded jeans and shirts so new she could see the creases from where they'd been folded around the cardboard inserts they'd been packaged with.

They were obviously starstruck, dazzled by the real live four-time Pro Rodeo bull-riding champion in their midst and, just as obviously, trying not to show it.

T-Bone was a lanky string bean of a cowboy with curly close-cropped hair, wild untamed eyebrows, and a wad of chew as big as a walnut bulging in his cheek. He was taciturn and often grumpy but he knew cattle and, thank God, had never shown any interest in running off to compete on the rodeo circuit. At least, not up to now, he hadn't. The way he was standing there, with his hands thrust into his back pockets, his head cocked attentively, nodding agreeably as he listened to whatever Clay was saying, made him look almost as starstruck as the two boys. Jo Beth decided she'd better nip that in the bud.

"I see you've met our new dude wrangler," she said to T-Bone as she approached the group.

T-Bone shot her a dubious glance. "Dude wrangler?"

"Yes. Clay here—" she tipped her head in his direction, as cool and composed as if they'd done nothing more in her office than discuss the terms of his employment "—has agreed to hire on for the summer to help me ride herd on our paying guests."

T-Bone raised his bushy brows, his expression conveying shocked skepticism and disgust in equal measures. "Better him than me," he said laconically, and spat out a stream of tobacco juice from between his front teeth.

Jo Beth frowned at the gob of brown goo on the ground between them. "You're going to have to watch that when the dudes get here," she said.

"They ain't here yet."

"They will be by tomorrow afternoon. And it won't make a very good first impression if one of them steps in a slimy wad of tobacco juice before they even get checked into their room."

"They don't want to step in anything slimy, they shouldn't be spendin' time on a cattle ranch."

One of the boys snickered.

Jo Beth turned a gimlet eye on him. "Did Miz Steele send you boys over?"

He sobered up immediately. "Yes, ma'am. We hitched a ride over with Clay. That is—" he amended, belatedly recalling his manners "—Mr. Madison."

"Clay's fine," Clay said.

Jo Beth ignored him. "And did she tell you what's expected of you?"

"Yes, ma'am. She said we was to give you a hand with whatever needed doing and if we caused any trouble she'd see to it that we regretted it."

"That about covers it," Jo Beth said approvingly. "You'll take your orders from T-Bone. What he says, goes. Is that clear?"

They nodded in unison. "Yes, ma'am."

"Take them to my office to fill out their withholding forms, then show them what needs doing," she said to T-Bone. "And make sure they head on back over to the Second Chance in time for their summer-school classes or Roxy will see to it that *I* regret it. You—" she jerked her chin at Clay "—come with me. I'll show you where you can park your rig." She walked around to the passenger side of his truck, pulled open the door, and climbed in. "Step on it, cowboy," she said when he took just a moment too long to answer her summons. "You've already wasted enough daylight."

Clay got into the truck. "You do know, don't you," he said, as he reached for the ignition, "that the dudes aren't going to be getting up at five o'clock? Or even six, probably. They're going to be on vacation. That means they're going to want to sleep in. Maybe have brunch out by the pool."

"You obviously haven't read our brochure. If you had, you'd know we offer our guests an authentic ranch experience. What that means, among other things, is three meals a day, served family-style in the dining room. Anyone who wants brunch is going to have to drive into town for it." She kept her voice and manner brisk and businesslike, the way she would with any new hand. It was best, she'd always thought, to begin as you meant to go on. And she meant, always, to have the upper hand.

"Head on around to the back side of the main barn," she said, directing him with a gesture. "We have electrical and water hookups you can use but no sewage facilities. So if you need to empty your blackwater tanks, you'll have to drive your rig on over to one of the RV and truck stations on 81."

Clay brought his rig—a black Chevy pickup and state-of-the-art fifth wheel trailer—to a stop in the spot she indicated, set the parking break, and turned off the ignition. Jo Beth had the door handle up before the engine stopped running, her right shoulder pressed against the door to shove it open. Clay reached out and grasped her forearm lightly, stopping her from exiting the cab.

Jo Beth froze in midmotion, and turned her head to look, first at his hand and then, her gaze traveling slowly up his arm, into his eyes. Her expression was faintly incredulous, as if she were a queen who couldn't believe one of her subjects had actually had the temerity to touch her. The look she gave him was the one he was beginning to think of as her freeze-the-balls-off-a-bull expression.

A lesser man would have been intimidated by that look and backed down. Clay merely tightened his grip on her arm and waited.

"You're crowding me again, cowboy," she said, her voice as frosty as her gaze. "And I believe I've already told you that I don't like to be crowded."

"Does that mean we're going to do it your way?"

"My way?"

"Strictly business?"

"No, it doesn't." Her eyes flashed sudden fire, a smoldering sensual heat, full of promise and challenge that caused him to loosen his grip in a way her icy glare hadn't. "But it also doesn't mean we're going to go at it in the front seat of this truck, either." She shook his hand off and slid out of the cab.

Clay sat where he was for a long moment, trying to get his bearings. She'd surprised him again, confused him, bemused and baffled him. The woman changed direction quicker than a Brahman bull, and her sudden moves left him just as off balance. More so actually, because he could usually sense which way a bull was going to jump and brace for it. With her, he realized, he didn't have a clue where things were going. She was fire and ice, then ice and fire, and sometimes both at the same time. It was maddening. And intriguing. And more challenging than anything had been in a long time. All he could do was hang on and ride it out, which, as luck would have it, was exactly what he liked best to do.

He was so immersed in trying to untangle the puzzle she presented that he jumped when she tapped on the glass on the driver's side door.

"We need to talk," she said, and motioned toward his trailer.

Had there ever been four words that struck more terror into the heart of man? he wondered, but he got out of the truck and followed her to the door of his fifth-wheeler. She stood wordlessly, waiting for him to unlock the door, and then preceded him inside. She moved to the middle of the trailer and then turned in a slow circle, her gaze openly assessing as she surveyed his home on wheels.

The interior was surprisingly clean and neat, with a place for everything and everything, apparently, in its place. There were no dirty dishes in the sink, no untidy piles of clothes on the floor, no objectionable "art" on the walls. In addition to an almost full-sized stainless steel sink, the kitchen consisted of a two-burner stove-top, a microwave, a miniature refrigerator, and a small built-in table with seating for four. A portable TV and a coffeemaker were attached to the underside of one of the cabinets, leaving the countertops free.

In place of the usual built-in sofa in the living area sat a complicated-looking exercise machine bristling with weights and pulleys. It was bolted to the floor, as was the weight bench next to it. A wooden bookcase with slats across the front of each shelf to keep the books from toppling out in transit took up the rest of the available space in the living area.

Through the partially opened pocket door at the front of the trailer, she could see a bed, neatly made, covered with a Navajo blanket in a zigzagging pattern in emerald green, black, and deep wine red. There was a piece of abstract art, vaguely western in design, made of hammered metal and polished wood, bolted to the wall above the bed. There were no rodeo posters, no display of trophy belt buckles, and absolutely no clutter.

It wasn't what she'd expected but, then, she couldn't really have said *what* she'd expected, except that she'd thought his living quarters would be more like him—brash, bold and unabashedly sexual. Instead, the trailer was poison neat, and nearly as austere as a monk's cell.

Her fingers itched to open the drawers and cupboards, to poke into cabinets and closets to see if that's where he kept the mess of his life. She leaned back against the kitchen counter instead, bracing her hips against it, and crossed her arms in front of her. "It's very nice."

"I like it." He raised an eyebrow at her. "But that's not what you brought me in here to talk about."

"No, it isn't." She shifted her stance, uncrossing her arms, and brought her hands down on either side of her hips, bracing them on the counter behind her.

"Why don't you quit fidgeting and just spit it out," he suggested. "Unless you'd rather I just hoist you up on that counter you're leaning on and do what we're both dying to do?"

She straightened away from the counter so fast an impartial observer might have thought one of the burners behind her had suddenly come on.

"I take it that means we're not going to 'go at it' in my trailer, either," he said.

"No, we're not."

"What then?"

Jo Beth took a deep breath and decided to just say it, straight out. That's what she was best at, after all. She was known for her bluntness and her ability to lay it— whatever *it* was—on the line.

"You were right," she said. "What we have is sex. Incredibly fantastic sex. And if you want to *keep* having it, it's got to be sex my way, by my rules."

"Which are?"

"There will be no hanky-panky in front of my guests or my other wranglers. No quickies in the barn or anywhere else we might get caught. No stolen kisses. No accidental little touches when you think no one's looking. None of those sly, knowing glances you think no one else sees. No slap-and-tickle in the front porch swing. No hand-holding. No butt patting. No pet names. No romantic nonsense of any kind. Just sex. And when it's over, it's over, and if I hear a whisper of gossip in the meantime, if I even *think* anyone suspects, it's over right then and there, and you're out of here. If you can't live with that, then you might as well climb back into the cab of your truck and head on down the road right now. Have I made myself clear?"

"As crystal," he said, surprised to find the words coming through clenched teeth. "Except for one thing."

"What's that?"

"Why?"

"Why what?"

"Why all the secrecy? What are you afraid of?"

"I'm not afraid of anything," she said. "I just like to keep my private life private, is all. I don't like being the subject of gossip. And I don't like sticky emotional strings. I like my sex easy and uncomplicated, with no commitments and no promises on either side."

"Like a man, you mean," he said, insulted. He wasn't quite sure what he was getting so riled about. She was offering him simple, undemanding, straightforward sex with no games and no strings and no obligations. He should be tickled pink. So why did he feel his hackles rising, like a dog who was being teased or a wolf sensing danger?

"Yes, *exactly* like a man," she said, pleased he understood. "Do we have a deal?" she asked, and stuck out her hand.

He looked at her from across the width of the narrow trailer, at her slim white hand, at her long silky brown braid and her big brown eyes, at the luscious swell of her shapely hips and the delicate curve of her small, stubborn chin. She was a hot, passionate, gorgeous woman, and she was offering him hot, passionate, uncomplicated sex. He'd be a stupid fool to say no.

"Deal," he said and reached out to take her hand in his.

8

SHE WENT TO HIM that night, very late, after the last light in the bunkhouse had flickered out and the bright silvery globe of a nearly full moon was riding high in the ink black sky. Millions of stars added their twinkling glow to the night, making the flashlight she carried unnecessary. She walked quietly but boldly out to the barn, using neither subterfuge nor stealth to camouflage her actions or direction. Although it was highly unlikely she'd be observed so late at night, anyone who happened to see her would assume she was on her way to the barn to check on one of the animals or simply taking a late night stroll. And no one would think to question her, anyway. She was, after all, the jefe of the Diamond J and it was her right to wander anywhere on the ranch, anytime she wanted to.

She moved into and through the dark, silent barn, her ears attuned by long custom to the soft snufflings and snores of sleeping livestock, the scuttling and scurrying of nighttime creatures, the creaking of old, weathered structures. She paused now and then to peek over a stall door at the animal inside—the pregnant mare that was near term, the Hereford cow that had cut itself on barbed wire and had needed stitching—assuring herself that all was well. Everything was quiet. Everything was as it should be.

She exited through a side door on the north end of the building and walked the remaining few yards across the open ground to Clay's trailer. The door was unlocked when she tried it. The inside of the trailer was dark and silent. She tiptoed carefully through the tiny living area and the galley-style kitchen, her hand outstretched, gingerly feeling her way along the countertop to the open pocket door at the front of the vehicle.

It was much lighter in the bedroom than in the rest of the trailer. There were long, narrow windows on either side of the bed, set high up in the walls for privacy. The short wine-red box-pleat curtains were pushed back, letting the moonlight stream in.

It spilled down on the recumbent form of the man in the bed. He was gloriously naked, a study in stark black and white in the moonlight, sprawled facedown on his stomach with the covers kicked off and lying in a heap at the foot of the bed. His head was pillowed on his right arm. His left knee was bent and drawn up nearly to his waist. The lighting and his position emphasized the long, smooth muscles of his back and legs, and the tight, startlingly white curve of his buttocks. It also exposed the tender, vulnerable flesh of his scrotum.

Jo Beth hovered in the open doorway, watching him, drinking him in with her eyes, feeling the wild, uncontrollable passion he roused in her rise up at the sight of him. She let it build until she couldn't wait one more minute, not one more second, to touch him. And then, stealthily, hurriedly she began to undress. Boots and jeans and a shirt were all she had on. She peeled them off as quietly as possible, turning to pile them on the kitchen counter behind her. Naked, she tiptoed into the bedroom and up to the edge of the bed. He was still sleeping. Or pretending to be asleep. Either way was fine with her.

She leaned over the bed and reached out, touching him, very lightly, with just the fingertips of her left hand. She drew them slowly from the nape of his neck, down the strong curving line of his spine, over the crease between his buttocks to the soft skin covering his testicles. She felt him raise his hips, just slightly—she knew he'd been playing opossum!—and she turned her hand, sliding it deeper between his legs, cupping him in her palm.

He made a soft murmuring noise, less than a moan, more than a sigh. She sat down on the edge of the bed and leaned over him, brushing her bare breasts against his back, continuing to caress his balls with her clever fingers, rolling them gently, back and forth, like delicate Ben-Wai balls in a fleshy sack.

"I'll give you about a year to stop that," he said, his voice already thick with lust. She felt his muscles bunch and tense as he started to roll over to give them both more room to play.

Jo Beth leaned more heavily into his back, holding him where he was, and put her lips to his ear. "Don't move," she said, and nipped his lobe, not quite gently, to reinforce her order.

He acquiesced immediately, relaxing onto the bed, silently ceding control to her. She sucked his earlobe into her mouth, flicking it with her tongue, then released it to draw a wet line down the side of his neck, to his nape, and down the hollow of his spine. She made her way down his back, slowly, with little cat licks, stopping now and then to blow gently on his skin, making him shiver in response. She kept the fingers of her left hand busy between his legs, gently squeezing and releasing his testicles as she licked her way down his back. She felt his body tense again as she drew near the base of his spine, but he lay very still and didn't so much as move a muscle.

She knew what he was waiting for, hoping for, what he was anticipating with every fiber of his being. She was anticipating it, too, and didn't make him wait, couldn't make him wait because it would mean that she had to wait, too. She withdrew her hand from between his legs and curved it around his hip. "Turn over now," she said, tugging a bit to make him roll onto his back.

His chest was wide and well developed, the smooth coil and flex of muscle and tendon shaded and defined beneath a dusting of fine silky hair that looked coalblack in the bright moonlight shining through the window. It grew in an almost perfect diamond pattern, starting from a point at the top of his sternum, spreading evenly from nipple to nipple and then narrowing down to a faint furry line that disappeared just a tad north of his belly button. His abdomen was washboard flat, roped with starkly defined muscles in the classic six-pack. His erection was massive in the moonlight, high and tight and hard against his washboard stomach.

Jo Beth shifted onto her knees beside his hip, slid her left hand down between his legs again to cup his balls, and curled her right around his cock, lifting it gently upright. Then she lowered her head, bringing her mouth down to within millimeters of his penis and swirled her tongue around the head, just once, as if she were licking a melting ice-cream cone.

His penis jerked in her hand and his whole body shuddered.

Jo Beth turned her head and gave him a little cat smile, rife with feminine knowledge and satisfaction at his helpless, heated response to her touch. "Don't move," she said softly, and then lowered her head and took him into her mouth.

His response was all she'd hoped for, all she'd wanted, all she'd fantasized about. His body stiffened and arched, taut as a bow beneath her ministering mouth. His hands fisted in the sheets beneath him. He whispered her name, softly at first, almost reverently, and then ever more frantically as her mouth called the passion from his body. He wasn't playing teasing sensual games now, he wasn't smug and cocksure and full of himself, he wasn't even thinking. He was pure, primal feeling, a man at his most elemental, helpless in his desperate desire for what she could give him.

Jo Beth was drunk on the power of her sensual appeal,

delirious with it, and determined to take it all the way. She was unwavering in her resolve to make him lose control the way she had lost it in Tom's tack room, dead set on making him tremble. And plead. And whimper.

The way she had trembled and pleaded and whimpered.

She sucked harder, taking more of him into her mouth on each down stroke, pressing her tongue firmly against the ultrasensitive vein on the underside of his shaft on the upstroke. The muscles in his taut stomach began to quiver. His legs twitched restlessly. His head rolled against the mattress.

She tugged on his testicles, pulling them gently away from his body, pressing two fingers against the supersensitive perineum just beneath.

"Oh, God, Jo. Yes. Please." His whole body strained upward. *"Please."*

He was on the edge, as she had been, wild with yearning, utterly frantic for release. She quickened the up-and-down movement of her head and felt the crown of his penis swell against her tongue, felt the drawing in and tightening of his scrotum against her caressing fingertips that signaled impending orgasm. He was very close. She increased her pace, relentlessly driving him to the finish.

"Sweet Jesus God!" The words were expelled on a breathless whimper as his body exploded in climax. She stayed with him, not lifting her head until the final orgasmic spasms racked his body.

He unclenched his fists and reached down with one

hand to touch the side of her face. "Jo," he said. His voice trembled. "Jo."

She turned her head, then, resting her cheek lightly against his half flaccid penis, and looked up at him.

"You didn't have to do that," he said.

"I wanted to. I've wanted to since practically the first minute I saw you. I've been *dying* to do that to you." She smiled lasciviously. "It's been one of my most persistent fantasies."

He knew she wasn't lying or exaggerating. She hadn't done it to please him or to placate him or to make him want her. She hadn't done it because she thought it was what *he* wanted, at all. That wasn't the kind of "relationship" they had; that wasn't the kind of woman she was. She'd done it to please herself, because it was what *she* wanted to do. He could only be grateful that he was the man she'd wanted to do it to—and with.

"Is there anything else you want to do? Any other fantasies I can help you fulfill?" He reached down, cupping her shoulders, and pulled her body up over his until they were face-to-face. He kissed her, a soft, nuzzling butterfly kiss. "Anything at all?"

"Well, now that you mention it…" She put her hands against his chest and pushed herself upright. Her legs slid down along either side of his waist. Her labia pressed against his belly. "What's your recovery time, cowboy?"

Amazingly, his recovery was already well underway. The second she'd straddled him and he'd felt her pussy, wet and aroused, against his belly, his penis had twitched and raised its head in renewed interest.

"What have you got in mind, boss?"

She grinned at him. "How do you feel about the woman-on-top position?"

"Right now, I'd say if the woman on top would slide her luscious little ass down about six inches, I'd feel just fine about it."

Jo Beth squirmed around on top of him, rubbing herself against him, moving down inch by exquisite inch until she felt the tip of his newly engorged penis prodding her equally engorged labia. She raised herself to her knees and reached down with one hand, intending to hold his penis upright so she could slide down on it. But Clay forestalled her. His hands were there first.

He placed his palms against the tops of her thighs. His fingers were curved outward, holding her in place above him, his thumbs were curved inward, touching her soft, wet pussy. He stroked her gently, easing open the slick folds of her body, following the petaled curves upward until his thumbs rested on either side of her clitoris. Squeezing lightly, he coaxed the tiny nubbin out from beneath its protective hood and then caressed it lightly, slowly, with short, languid upward strokes, alternating thumbs so that one caress was barely over before the next began.

Jo Beth shuddered and started to lean forward to brace her hands on his chest, but that would have dislodged his thumbs. She leaned backward instead, bracing her hands behind her on his thighs. The position arched her body, pushing her breasts out and giving him better access for his busy hands. He widened his field of attack, sliding his hands up her body to her breasts, flicking her nipples lightly, pinching them, then sliding his hands back down again to resume his sensual assault on the throbbing nubbin of flesh between her legs. It went on for several long, delicious minutes, the languorous slip and slide of his hands making their slow, maddening trek up and down her body, stroking and caressing, pinching and tugging, inflaming her, arousing her, driving her mad.

Jo Beth's breathing gradually came faster and harsher, until she was panting lightly. She began to tremble, her arms, her belly, her legs, all shaking so badly she could barely hold herself upright. The red flush of impending orgasm covered her breasts and upper torso.

"Oh, God. I can't." Her voice was as shaky as her body as she struggled to hold herself upright. "Please, Clay. I'm falling apart. I can't."

He slid his hands from her thighs to her waist, pulling her upright so that she was, once again, balanced on her knees over him. "Give me a second," he said, his voice nearly as shaky as hers as he reached under the pillow for one of the condoms he'd stashed there earlier. Quickly he tore it open and sheathed himself, then reached for her again.

He cupped his hands around the backs of her knees and then moved down her calves to her ankles. He pulled her feet forward gently, guiding them around his waist as he sat up. He wrapped one arm around her, lifting her up as he shifted his legs. When he eased her back down again, she slid smoothly onto his penis. The snug heat of her vagina gripped him like a glove. The hard length of his cock stretched and filled her. She shuddered and sighed and settled onto him, lifting her hands to his shoulders to keep her exactly where she was, exactly where she wanted to be.

They sat face-to-face, breast-to-chest, groin-to-groin, man-to-woman. Her legs were wrapped around his waist, her ankles locked at the small of his back. His legs were crossed loosely behind her, his heels pressing into the crease of her buttocks to provide support and keep her from rolling backward and losing their connection. He rocked back and forth, slowly, rhythmically, providing just enough friction to keep her on the screaming edge of release but not quite enough to send her over it.

"Have you ever tried tantric sex?"

Jo Beth shook her head. "No."

"Would you like to?"

"Is that what we're doing?"

"Not exactly." He stopped moving. "The purpose of tantric sex is to try *not* to have an orgasm."

"Try *not* to have an orgasm?" Jo Beth said incredulously. She wanted an orgasm so bad, she was almost ready to beg for one, scream for one, demand one. "Why would anyone try not to have an orgasm?"

"It's like when somebody tells you not to think about pink elephants." He smiled into her eyes. "From that moment on, all you can think about is pink elephants. Big, fluffy pink elephants. So, when I tell you not to have an orgasm…"

"I have an orgasm?"

His lips curved up in a seductive smile. "Eventually."

She pouted. "I want one now."

"Eventually." He smoothed his big hands down the length of her back, his fingertips grazing the delicate bumps of her spine, and cupped her bottom, one cheek of her ass in each wide palm. He tilted her pelvis forward, slightly, changing the angle and the pressure of their connection.

Heat sizzled through her like forked lightning. She gasped and closed her eyes, straining for the release that hovered just over the edge of sensation.

"Don't have an orgasm," he said, "and open your eyes."

She lifted her lashes and glared at him, her mutinous expression only half-counterfeit. "I want to come. I *need* to come."

"It'll be better if you wait."

"That's easy for you to say. You've already had yours."

"And you'll get yours, too. I promise. And it will be spectacular. The longer you wait, the more spectacular it will be. In the meantime—" he ran his hands down to her butt again, tilted her forward, rocked her against him until she shuddered "—enjoy the journey. And open your eyes. Look at me while I'm driving you crazy."

She waited until the almost-orgasm slipped irrevocably away and then lifted her lashes again. Her expression was soft and tumultuous, heavy with unsatisfied desire, drowsy with sensuality. His was intense and focused and powerfully, keenly aroused. He held her gaze with his, staring deeply into her eyes, watching her passion rise and fall and rise again as she reacted to the slow, hypnotic stroking of his hands as he skimmed them over her body, barely touching.

He grazed her strong, supple shoulders and back, the narrow slope of her waist, the enticing swell of her hips. He traced the long, firm muscles of her widespread thighs with his fingertips, down along the outside of her legs to her knees and then back up, his hands floating along her inner thighs, briefly touching the place where they were joined. His fingers skimmed the soft, slippery flesh stretched so tightly around him, and then back up again, over her flat, quivering belly, around and around her breasts, barely brushing her nipples, and back up to her shoulders to start the exquisite torture all over again.

"I promised you hours," he said, his voice low and hot and crooning. He rocked her limp, heated body against him. "I can give you hours like this."

"I can't take hours like this." Despite her melting pliancy, every nerve ending in her body was strung tight, humming with exquisite anticipation, drowning in languorous, lubricous need. "Hours like this would kill me." She let her head fall back with a ragged, whimpering sigh. "I'm dying now."

He caught her head in one hand and moved the other to the middle of her back, keeping her from melting into a boneless puddle on the bed. "Don't have an orgasm," he crooned low, calling her back from the edge of the abyss. "And open your eyes."

She groaned in frustration and opened her eyes. "Bastard," she said. The word was a caress and a taunt, accolade, and reprimand all rolled into one. "You're a cruel, devious, conniving, unfeeling bastard, and I hate you."

"Yep, I'm a bastard, all right." He grinned. It was his slow, I'm-all-that-and-more cowboy grin. "And you're hotter and wetter than you've ever been before, aren't you? You're so hot you're burning up from the inside out." He shifted his hands to her waist and let her fall a little farther back, so that her spine was arched in a graceful bow and her pelvis was pressed more tightly against his. "Aren't you?" he demanded.

"Yes. Oh, God, yes."

"You're primed to explode."

"Yes."

"Just the slightest touch, the slightest movement, in just the right way, will set you off."

"Yes. Oh, please, yes."

She hung there between his hands like a rag doll, her back arched, her breasts out-thrust, her thighs wide-spread, the small soft sensitive opening to her vagina taut and tight around him. He lifted her slightly, pulling her toward him with his hands on her waist, then let her fall back down. Lifted. Let her fall. Lifted…

It was hardly any movement at all, just the tiniest hint of friction, barely qualifying as a thrust, but it was exactly where she needed it. It was exactly enough. Exactly right.

The sensation it created was agonizingly pleasurable and unbearably intense, and she couldn't take it one minute longer, not one second. She was going to explode all over him. She was going to come so deep and so hard...

"Open your eyes, Jo Beth." He lifted her just a little higher, slid her up his shaft just a little farther, increased the friction just a little more. "I want to watch you when you come. I want you to watch me watching you."

She opened her eyes. They were ablaze with helpless passion, her pupils dilated so that her soft-brown irises looked inky-black in the moonlight. And then, suddenly, inevitably, the feeling twisting her nerves into heated screaming knots crested. She hovered there for a long excruciating, exquisite moment, trembling on the brink of satisfaction. He tightened his hands on her waist, pulling her down tight against him with a hard little rotating motion that ground their pubic bones together. The tension in her body imploded with staggering force. Her eyes went blank with pleasure. She gave a low guttural groan that sounded as if it had been ripped from her body and slipped over the edge of reason into pure physical sensation.

Clay gathered her up against his chest, holding her close and safe as the aftershocks shuddered through her. She was utterly, completely limp with pleasure, exhausted, overwhelmed, helpless. She made no protest when he nuzzled her neck, didn't turn away when he kissed her eyelids and her forehead and her cheeks, voiced no objections when he tucked her securely against his side.

Clay's own raging orgasm, experienced in the moments just after she reached her final peak, went almost unnoticed, overshadowed and eclipsed by the triumph of hers.

9

CLAY TOLD HIMSELF that the faint niggling sensation of discontent he felt when he woke up alone the next morning was nothing more than disappointment at not being able to indulge in a playful bout of morning sex. After all, morning sex was one of his favorite activities. He liked women who were bed-warmed and sleepy-eyed. He liked them with their hair tousled and their makeup gone. He liked waking them up with little baby kisses and sneaky under-the-cover caresses that had them aroused and willing before they were fully awake. He liked it when they giggled and squirmed because his morning stubble was scratchy. And he *really* liked it when they could be convinced—and they usually could be—to join him in his morning shower for a second go-round. That sort of action always started his day off right.

Not that Jo Beth struck him as a giggler. In fact, she'd probably have pushed him away and told him in no uncertain terms in that deliciously snooty I'm-the-boss-and-don't-you-forget-it tone of hers to go shave before he came near her. But then—he grinned into his pillow at the thought—with all of his considerable determination and extensive sexual expertise, he could have convinced her she really didn't mean that.

Just like she hadn't meant it last night when she'd called him a bastard in that sulky sex-kitten voice that was so at odds with the one she usually used. His grin widened at the memory of her sitting hot and naked in his lap with her long lithe legs wrapped around his waist and her firm, slender body limp with desire between his hands. Unlike most women he'd known, who could barely string two coherent words together when he had them in that position, Jo Beth had glared at him through passion-drugged eyes and managed to deliver an entire sentence that succinctly conveyed her annoyance with him and his tormenting sex play. Of course, it'd only taken him about two minutes to change her mind and have her writhing and melting and purring in his arms. A good, heart-stopping orgasm tended to do that to a woman.

He was confident he could have gotten around the morning-beard problem just as easily if she'd stayed. Of course, even if she had, it was doubtful she'd be lolling around in bed with him. Despite her adventurous sexual appetites and the obvious pleasure she derived from indulging them, Jo Beth was a nose-to-the-grindstone, no-nonsense type of woman who jumped out of bed at first light without waiting to see if it might be more fun to sleep in.

Speaking of which, he was pretty sure it was first light he saw creeping around the edges of the pillow he had mashed over his face. He yanked it off his head, tossing it to the floor with the covers he'd lost sometime last night, and squinted at the bedside clock bolted to his nightstand. The bright red numerals read 4:45. If he wanted to impress the jefe of the Diamond J with something other than his sexual prowess—and he damned well did—it was time to haul his ass out of bed.

Jo Beth woke the next morning, sleepy-eyed and a bit groggy, her body feeling deliciously relaxed and loose and supple. She stretched her arms over her head and yawned hugely, feeling like Scarlett O'Hara the night after Rhett Butler had carried her up the stairs and had his wicked way with her. A satisfied little grin curled the corners of her mouth as she gazed up at the yellow paint on the ceiling of her bedroom. It was amazing what a good orgasm—or two or three—could do for a woman's mood. And Clay Madison gave damned good orgasms.

She wondered if he were awake yet, if he had awoken, as she had, feeling the distinct need for more of the same pleasure they had shared last night. She didn't usually wake up horny—not that it would do her any good if she did, anyway, because she could count on the fingers of one hand the number of times she'd greeted the morning with a man in her bed—but this morning, well, the itch between her legs would have had her straddling her fantasy cowboy to scratch it before she crawled out of bed to face the rest of her day.

She lay there for another moment, contemplating scratching it herself. It would only take a couple of minutes to achieve release but, hell, fantasy sex and self-gratification would doubtless only provide the same fleeting satisfaction she'd experienced in the water tank. Especially now that she had the reality to compare it to and knew, without a doubt, that her fantasies didn't even come *close* to the reality of Clay Madison.

He'd spoiled her for fantasy, just as she was afraid he might spoil her for other men.

She sighed at the thought and deliberately pushed it out of her mind. It was an idiotic thought, anyway. Men were men, and sex was sex, and both were readily available to pretty much any woman who went looking for them. After Clay Madison had packed up and headed on down the road out of her life, she'd take a good look around her and find someone else to accommodate her sexual needs. There were plenty more where he came from. Plenty.

She sighed again and frowned up at the ceiling. Just contemplating the need to find another discreet, compatible, inventive sex partner when Clay was gone had taken the edge off her morning desire and spoiled her good mood. She might as well crawl out from under the covers and get a head start on the day. There was a whole heap of a lot still to get done before the first dudes arrived that afternoon. She threw back the single sheet and thin blanket covering her and swung her feet to the floor, glancing at the old-fashioned brass windup alarm clock on her nightstand as she did so. What she saw had her swearing a blue streak and racing for the bathroom. It was nearly 7:00 a.m.

"*BUENOS DÍAS.*" Esperanza glanced up from her work-table and smiled a greeting at Jo Beth as she hurried into the kitchen. "The coffee is still hot on the stove." The housekeeper gestured toward it with a tilt of her head, her busy hands pat-pat-patting corn dough into tortillas. "And there are muffins in the basket on the counter. I will cook you some eggs when I have finished with this tortilla."

"No, don't bother, please, Esperanza. I haven't got time for a regular breakfast this morning. I'm expecting the pool guy to arrive any minute." She grabbed a heavy white ceramic mug from the cupboard above the tiled counter and filled it with coffee as she spoke. "Coffee and a muffin will have to do me until lunch."

"The man from the swimming pool company is already here," Esperanza said, "and lunch is a long time away. You need to eat."

Jo Beth paused with her hand poised over the basket of muffins. "He's already here?"

"*Sí.*"

"Well, why didn't you say so?" She turned from the basket of muffins without taking one. "Where is he?"

"He is out looking at the swimming pool. Señor Clay is with him."

"Clay's with him? Why is Clay with him?"

"Señor Clay is our new 'dude wrangler,' *sí?*" Esperanza said, stumbling a bit over the unfamiliar term. "Is it not his *trabajo*…his job…to look after all that will concern our guests when they arrive?"

"No." Jo Beth set her mug of coffee on the counter with a sharp little click. "It most certainly is not his job."

"It is not?" Esperanza said, but Jo Beth was already headed out the back door.

The minute she stepped out onto the back porch of the ranch house, she saw him. He was standing on the pebbled concrete patio surrounding the newly filled swimming pool with T-Bone and a young man in khaki shorts and a sky-blue knit pullover shirt with the pool company name artistically scrawled across the back of it. They appeared to be deep in conversation, all three heads bent over something in Clay's hand. She couldn't quite make out what it was.

They made quite an incongruous little group, with the pool guy looking like a California surfer who'd gotten lost on the way to the beach, and T-Bone and Clay in full cowboy regalia, including chaps.

Looking at Clay's admittedly delectable rear view, Jo Beth had a sudden recollection of the stripper at Cassie's bachelorette party, bumping and grinding around the room wearing chaps and a G-string. She wondered if she could convince Clay to wear a similar outfit—minus the G-string. Just the thought made her smile.

And then Clay looked up and caught sight of her, standing there on the porch, and raised his arm to wave her on down. She wiped the dopey smile off her face, replacing it with what she hoped was her usual dour expression, and made her way down the back steps and across the patch of newly sodded lawn to the pool area.

"Mornin', boss," Clay said. The smile he gave her was open and friendly with absolutely no hint of familiarity or sexuality—at least, no more than was usual for him.

Something in Jo Beth relaxed infinitesimally as something she hadn't even known was worrying her let go and disappeared into the hot Texas sunshine. She had been afraid—and hadn't even known she'd been afraid—that he would somehow, someway, manage to broadcast their relationship. That he would, with sly innuendo or heated looks or a macho display of that aggravating proprietary air some men adopted toward the women they had sex with, manage to convey to all and sundry that he was sleeping with her.

It was, she realized, an unworthy suspicion on her part. He'd given absolutely no indication that he was the type to kiss and tell. She felt just the least bit apologetic for even thinking he might be. As a result, her answering smile was as open and friendly as his.

"What have you got there?" she asked, with a nod at the item in his hand.

"It's the pool test kit," the pool guy said before Clay could answer. "I was just showing your 'dude wrangler' here—" he grinned at the term "—how to use it."

T-Bone was grinning, too, or as close to it as he ever got. His tobacco-stained gap-toothed grimace let her know that he was the one who'd made sure everyone knew Clay's "official" job designation. Jo Beth was suddenly sorry she'd ever coined the term. She should have known it would come back to bite her in the ass.

"Listen, guys, let's cool it with the 'dude wrangler' bit, okay?" She softened the order with a smile. "I don't want the dudes hearing themselves referred to as anything but guests."

"That mean Clay's the *guest* wrangler, then?" T-Bone asked.

"How 'bout we call him our… Oh, I don't know… Social director?" Jo Beth suggested.

Clay grinned. "Does that mean I have to plan parties and arrange shuffleboard games?"

"We don't have shuffleboard but, yes, I guess it does mean you'll be lending a hand with the parties."

Clay's grin faded into something very much like shock. He'd been kidding. "You actually throw parties for the du—er, guests?"

"Chuck-wagon night," T-Bone informed him gleefully, and pursed his lips to spit.

"T-Bone William McGuire, don't you dare spit tobacco juice on my new concrete patio!"

Jo Beth's words stopped him cold, causing him to clamp his lips shut and stare at her with a desperate look that silently asked what he was supposed to do with a mouthful of chew that needed to be spit out.

"You've got two choices. Three, if you're smart," she said. "Swallow it—"

"Ah, ma'am—" the pool guy interrupted. "He swallows it, it'll make him sick as a dog. And then you'll have an even bigger mess on the patio."

Jo Beth froze him with a look that said, plainly, butt out. She'd been around cowboys all her life. She knew what swallowing chew would do. She'd swallowed a mouthful of it herself when she was nine.

"You swallow it," she said, turning her attention back to T-Bone. His face was turning an interesting shade of green and his eyes were beginning to bulge. "Or you start carrying around your own personal spittoon. Or you quit. I'd suggest quitting."

T-Bone mumbled something from behind his closed lips, clamped a hand over his mouth, and took off at a fast trot toward the barn. He made it as far as the first line of scrub oaks that acted as a windbreak between the outbuildings and the main house. And then he bent over, one hand braced against a gnarled tree, and puked up his breakfast.

"You be sure and clean up after yourself," Jo Beth hollered at him. "I don't want that mess lying around for one of our guests to step in."

"Oh, you're mean." Clay shook his head mournfully. "Poison mean." A small smile curved his lips. "I like that in a woman."

"Well, stick around, then, cowboy, 'cause I can get a lot meaner when I have to." She glanced back toward the line of trees, her expression giving away her concern for the cowhand. T-Bone was standing upright, wiping his mouth with the blue bandanna from around his neck.

"Maybe he'll actually quit this time," she said, half to herself, and then, satisfied the cowhand was all right, she turned her attention back to Clay and the pool man. "Show me how that works," she demanded, jerking her chin at the pool test kit.

THE FIRST CONTINGENT of dudes—*guests,* Jo Beth reminded herself—arrived midday in a gleaming white SUV that was covered with a fine layer of dust and grit by the time it had made the half mile trek up the long graveled driveway from the main road to the ranch house. Jo Beth stood on the front porch, her hand tented over her eyes, watching the SUV bump its way down the road. Her stomach was tied in knots, and what little bit wasn't in knots was being attacked by crazed butterflies.

She'd sunk a heap of money into this new venture and if it didn't pay off, she was going to be in a heap of trouble financially. She'd have to sell more land to cover her losses and if she did that the Diamond J would go from being a good medium-sized Texas spread to little more than a hobby farm.

The ranch was already less than it had been in her daddy's and granddaddy's day, but after her father's death two years ago, there'd been a mountain of medical bills to pay and her mother wanted to retire to the coast and get away from ranching altogether. So Jo Beth had bitten the bullet, sold off enough land and cattle to pay off the bills and set her mother up in a nice little condo in Galveston. She'd used what was left to make the improvements necessary to open the place to vacationers.

Dude ranching was big business in many ranching communities, and paying guests were what enabled lots of ranchers all over the West to afford to *stay* in the ranching business. She was hoping it would do the same for her. It wasn't a perfect solution, and not one that she would have chosen if she'd had her druthers, but it was one that had proved workable for lots of other ranchers. She had high hopes that it would work for her, too. Her entire first season was already booked solid. Now all she had to do was make sure nothing went wrong and the dudes liked what she offered them enough to come back and to tell their friends about the Diamond J.

According to the literature she'd received from the Dude Ranchers' Association, repeat customers and positive word of mouth were what made operations like hers successful.

For Jo Beth, success would mean that the Diamond J would still be, first and foremost, a working cattle ranch. If her plans failed and the new operation wasn't the success she'd hoped it would be, she didn't know what she'd do. Ranching was all she knew. It was what she loved. There was no place else she wanted to be. Nothing else she'd rather do.

The Diamond J Dude Ranch and Family Resort *had* to be a success. Nothing else was acceptable.

The SUV pulled to a stop in the driveway and city slickers Ted and Carla Branson and their two young sons stepped out onto the sun-baked yard of the Diamond J. Jo Beth plastered a wide, welcoming smile on her face, mentally gathering herself together, and prepared to step down off the porch to welcome her first paying guests.

Clay put a hand on her arm. "Take a deep breath," he said. "And stop gritting your teeth like that or you'll scare 'em off. You look demented."

Jo Beth turned her head to glare at him, but he'd already moved past her, down the wide wooden front steps, his hand held out as he approached the driver's side of the SUV.

"Howdy there, Mr. Branson." He clasped the hand of the stocky red-haired man who'd gotten out of the driver's side of the vehicle and then turned and shook the hand of the man's petite blond wife as she came around the front of the SUV from the other side. "Mrs. Branson." He pumped her hand once and let it go. "Welcome to the Diamond J. I'm Clay Madison, the head dude wrangler."

His charming cowboy grin was as wide and open as the Texas sky, inviting them to share the joke. Mr. and Mrs. Branson grinned back at him, obviously delighted to do so.

"What that means is I'm in charge of making sure y'all have a real good time." He reached back and clamped a hand on the sleeve of Jo Beth's blue chambray shirt, yanking her forward. "This here is Miz Jo Beth Jensen. She's the jefe of the Diamond J, and your hostess while you're vistin' with us. Her job is to make sure you see what real ranchin' is like."

Jo Beth came forward to shake hands and offer her own more restrained, though she fervently hoped, no less warm, welcome. It was easier now that Clay had broken the ice. She would have been stiff, she knew, and chilly, and would probably have put them off, which would have set the wrong tone and made things awkward. But Clay had put them all at ease and in a cheerful mood, making them ready to enjoy themselves and have fun.

"What's a hef-ay?"

Clay turned to see the two youngest Bransons staring up at him. They both had thick bright red hair, a face full of freckles and shockingly blue eyes. They were about seven or eight years old. Twins, he thought, or so close in age and looks that it made no difference. They were staring up at him with wide-eyed admiration and awe. The last person who'd looked at him like that had been considerably older and female—and naked, to boot—but it was a look he recognized, whatever the source.

He grinned at them. "Jefe means boss in Spanish," he said.

"Is that lady your boss?"

"Yes, indeed, she surely is. She's the boss of everybody here. She's the owner of the Diamond J."

"Are you a real cowboy?" asked the other little boy.

"I sure am."

"Do you have a horse?"

Clay decided it was probably best not to burst their bubble. "He's over there, yonder, in the barn," he said, pointing.

"What's his name?"

"Ah—" Clay had to think fast. "Blackie." That had been the name of his first horse back on his parents' ranch in Nebraska. There was probably a horse on the Diamond J with that name, too. It was a common equine moniker.

"Can we ride him?"

"We've got lots of horses you can ride."

"Have you got cows?"

"Yep." Clay nodded. "Lots of cows. Hundreds. We've even got some brand-new baby cows you can look at. 'Ceptin' we call 'em calves, here'bouts."

"Can we pet them?"

"Well, I don't know about that. Sometimes the mama cows don't like anyone to touch their babies. We'll have to ask Miz Jo what she thinks."

"Because she's the hef-ay?"

"That's right. And what she says, goes."

"And you got to do what she tells you to do."

"Yep. I've got to do whatever she tells me to do."

Clay heard a warm feminine chuckle. "Lucky girl," Carla Branson said.

Clay shot her a rogue's grin, acknowledging the compliment, even as a new sense of caution had him reconsidering the wisdom of his words. "I didn't mean that the way it might have sounded, ma'am," he said politely, shooting a wary glance at Jo Beth.

She was talking to Carla Branson's husband about the available fishing in the area and the possibility of hunting for fossils or arrowheads, and hadn't heard him.

Carla Branson waved a hand. "I didn't mean what I said the way it might have sounded, either," she assured him. "I was just making a comment. And not a very clever one, at that, apparently."

"Mom. Mom." One of the boys tugged on the hem of her blouse. "Mom. This man's a real cowboy."

"Yes, I can see that."

"He has a horse and everything."

"He said we could ride it," the other boy said. "Can we ride it, Mom?"

"Later." She put a hand on each boy's shoulder, turning them both toward the open door to the back seat of the SUV as she spoke. "We need to unload the car first and get settled into our rooms. Get your jackets and your video games." She gave them both an encouraging nudge. "We'll see about horseback riding after you get unpacked."

"But, Mo-o-o-m..." the whine began.

"Zac. Spencer." Their father's voice cut the whine in half. "Mind your mother."

"Clay will make sure your luggage gets to your rooms." Jo Beth said. "So, please, just leave it here by the car and come with me. I'll show you the way." She extended her hand, indicating that they should take the winding gravel path that wound around the side of the main house. The two boys ran on ahead, shepherded closely by their father, who had to break into a trot to keep up with them.

Carla Branson's progress was considerably less hurried than her menfolks' and Jo Beth deliberately altered her pace to accommodate the other woman's leisurely stroll.

"I take it our rooms aren't in the ranch house?" Carla Branson said.

"No, they aren't," Jo Beth answered nervously, hoping she hadn't just made her first error as an hotelier. "I've put you in what used to be the foreman's cabin. I thought, with the boys, you'd want connecting bedrooms. The only ones we have in the main house are two singles on the second floor with a bathroom in between. They're not very big, but, if you'd like, I can arrange to have your things put there instead."

"No, I'm sure whatever arrangements you've made will be fine. It's just that the main house is so gracious and charming."

Jo Beth darted a quick look at the house she'd grown up in, trying to see it through Carla Branson's eyes. It had always been just home to her. She'd never thought of it as either gracious or charming. It surprised her to realize that it was both of those things, especially with the new coat of paint—gleaming white on the clapboard siding and glossy black on the shutters—and the new landscaping. There was a bit of green lawn now and healthy shrubs along the foundation below the porch railing, where before there had been only scrub grass and a weed-grown bed of struggling flowers. Cascading red geraniums in moss-lined wire baskets hung at intervals along the porch overhang, shaded from the worst of the midday sun. There was an old-fashioned wooden swing with green-and-white-checked gingham cushions and two rocking chairs on the refinished front porch.

"It's not at all what I expected a Texas ranch house to look like," Carla said.

Jo Beth flashed the woman her first unforced smile of the day. "You were expecting the Ponderosa, weren't you? Something made out of great big rough-hewn logs?"

Carla Branson chuckled. "'Fraid so." Her blue eyes twinkled. "How'd you know?"

"Even as old as it is, that TV show is most people's only exposure to ranch life. Most Texas ranch houses are just like this one, though, especially in the hill country. Wooden clapboard siding. A gabled roof." She gestured toward the house as she spoke. "A wide wraparound porch to keep the sun out as much as possible. Down in southwest Texas you'll find some adobes with red tile roofs. But you have to head a lot farther north, all the way to Wyoming and Montana, or out west to Nevada before you find very many ranch houses made out of logs."

"Well, it's lovely," Carla Branson said.

"The foreman's cabin is the same style," Jo Beth assured her. "It's just smaller in scale. It has two bedrooms with a living area in between, and a mini-kitchen with a stovetop and a refrigerator, which I thought might come in useful if your boys want a snack."

"My boys *always* want a snack," Carla said.

"Oh, wow, a pool!" they heard one of the boys shout gleefully. A moment later, the rapid pounding of sneakered feet brought both boys streaking back around the corner of the house to their mother. "Mom, they've got a pool! They've got a pool!" they shrieked, grabbing hold of her hands to drag her the rest of the way.

Jo Beth quickened her pace to keep up.

"Just like in the brochure," she heard their mother say. "Change into your bathing suits, boys, and we'll take a swim before dinner."

For the first time since she started her new venture,

Jo Beth really, truly began to believe that it just might prove successful, after all.

BY FOUR O'CLOCK all the guests with reservations for the first week of operation had arrived. Esperanza and one of her nieces, who'd been hired to help provide waitressing and maid service, provided a delicious welcome buffet supper on the poolside patio. The guests feasted on authentic Mexican *especialidads,* including shredded pork tamales baked in corn husks, enchiladas made with handmade tortillas and fresh salsa, and cinnamon *sopaipillas,* deep-fried puff pastry drizzled with honey, for dessert.

By ten o'clock all the guests were safely tucked away in their rooms. The four Bransons were securely ensconced in the former foreman's cabin, which had previously been Jo Beth's living quarters from the time she returned home from college to take on the foreman's job herself until she began the renovations nearly a year ago to add guest facilities to the ranch.

A divorced father and his sulky fourteen-year-old son were in the two single dormer rooms on the second floor with the connecting bathroom in between.

A young married couple celebrating their first wedding anniversary occupied the third upstairs bedroom and the bathroom connected to it.

Two bright, pretty New York City twenty-somethings, whom—judging by the shameless way they'd flirted with all the cowhands—Jo Beth suspected of harboring some hot cowboy fantasies of their own, were sharing the big front bedroom and bath on the first floor, which had been Jo Beth's parents' room.

And Jo Beth was tucked into a small bedroom at the back of the house in a space that had once been the laundry porch way back before the house had been wired for electricity in the early 1900s. It had served mainly as a storage area since then and had been turned into her private retreat during the renovations. It was a long, fairly narrow room, with enough space for a bed at one end and a sitting area at the other. It had a tiny bathroom in one corner, only big enough for a commode, a sink, and a shower stall. It also had a door that opened to the outside.

Jo Beth didn't even wait for all the lights to flicker out before she eased the door open and headed down to the trailer parked behind the barn.

10

JUST LIKE THE NIGHT BEFORE, the door to the trailer was unlocked. Unlike the night before, however, Clay wasn't waiting naked in bed for her. He was in the shower. Steam billowed out of the open bathroom door, filling the air with moist heat and the clean, woodsy fragrance of pine-scented soap.

She thought about joining him—the open door was surely an invitation—but decided to wait. She'd seen his bathroom the previous evening. The shower stall was barely big enough for him to stand in without banging his elbows on the walls. One of them would get hurt if they tried to engage in any kind of soapy sexual fun in the tiny cubicle. Besides, she'd already washed, dried and rebraided her hair and she didn't want to get it wet again; the thick, wavy mass took forever to dry.

From the look of things, she assumed he'd been working out, though why he'd need more exercise after the nonstop sixteen-hour day he'd already put in escaped her. In any case, there was a set of dumbbells on the floor next to the weight bench, and the complicated arrangement of weights and pulleys on the exercise machine was set in a different configuration than it had been the last time she'd seen it. A damp towel had been spread over one of the machine's crossbars to dry. She pulled it off the bar and held it to her nose. It smelled of hot, hardworking male and something else less pleasant. She sniffed again, more gingerly. The scent of analgesic ointment made her wrinkle her nose and return the towel to its spot.

She wondered what kind of pain he was in, and if it was bad. Or, rather, how bad it was. She knew rodeo cowboys, like other professional athletes in rough contact sports—and rodeo was one of the roughest—were almost always in some kind of pain, nursing a pulled muscle or a bruised rib or just feeling the general achiness that came from being banged around all the time. The most successful rodeo cowboys, the ones who survived the game the longest and won the most trophy money and big, shiny belt buckles, had an unusually high tolerance for pain. But a high tolerance didn't mean they didn't feel it, especially when it was the kind of pain that came from the crisscrossing network of scars that marred Clay's perfect body.

They mostly ran up and down his right leg, from his groin to just past his knee, but there were a few low on his abdomen, too. They were new scars, still faintly pink in places, hard to see clearly in the moonlight, no matter how bright. She'd seen enough last night to know, though, that they were an ugly mishmash of precise surgical incisions and jagged wounds inflicted by the hooves and horns of an enraged Brahman bull. He had ignored them, so she'd done him the courtesy of ignoring them, too, but she couldn't help but wonder at the toll they had taken—and continued to take—on him.

She heard the shower stop. "Hey, cowboy," she called out, letting him known he wasn't alone in the trailer.

He poked his head out, peering around the edge of the open door. "Hey, yourself." He grinned at her. "Why didn't you join me? I left the door open."

Jo Beth shook her head. "There isn't enough room in your shower for what would have happened if I'd joined you."

"Is, too," he said with mock petulance, giving a dead-on impersonation of the Branson brothers. The two boys had been overtired from the long trip to the Diamond J and had gotten overexcited roughhousing in the pool. Their mother had finally had to separate them to stop their bickering and ended up putting them to bed as soon as supper was over.

Jo Beth smiled at him. "I know what you're up to," she said, "but I'm not quite ready to put you to bed yet."

His eyes lit up with the sensual interest that was never far from the surface. "You got something else planned?"

"I might," she teased.

"What?"

"Dry off that gorgeous body and come out here and I'll show you."

He grinned again. "Give me one minute," he said, and disappeared back into the bathroom.

He was already more or less dry but he grabbed a towel from the bowl of the sink where he'd dropped it and began the process all over again. It wasn't as if he was stalling, exactly, and it wasn't because *he* was sensitive about his scars. It was just that some women, when they saw his leg in the bright light tended to turn squeamish on him, or get all fussy and sympathetic, or ask a lot of fool questions he didn't want to answer.

Not that he thought Jo Beth would get squeamish. She was a rancher and ranchers, by definition, were not squeamish people, even when they were female. She probably wasn't going to go all fussy and sentimental on him, either, because Jo Beth was one of the least fussy women he'd ever known. And if she hadn't asked a lot of fool questions last night, it stood to reason that she wouldn't now.

He caught his own gaze in the mirror. "Okay," he said to his reflection. "So maybe I'm a *little* sensitive."

It wasn't something he liked to admit, even to himself. Especially to himself. He wrapped the towel around his waist, knotting it low on his left hip, and swaggered out of the tiny bathroom just to prove he wasn't all *that* sensitive about it.

Jo Beth was sitting on the end of the padded weight bench, bare-legged, wearing one of his black western snap-front shirts and a sly, sexy smile on her face. His chaps were draped across her lap. He recognized them by the distinctive row of silver conchas running down each leg.

He eyed her warily, suspicious of that smile. "What are you planning to do with those?"

"Nothing." She stroked a hand over the smooth, worn leather. "Yet."

"Yet?" He leaned against the kitchen counter and crossed his arms over his wide, bare chest. The pose was casual and lazily arrogant and, Jo Beth realized, it took most of his weight off of his right leg. It abruptly occurred to her that his regular stance, hipshot, casual, with his left foot flat on the ground and his right knee slightly bent, did the same thing.

It could, of course, be the way he had always stood, or it could be an unconscious accommodation to the pain he constantly battled.

She ran her gaze down the long length of his body, from the smoothly rounded muscles in his bare shoulders and hair-dusted chest, to the bugling biceps of his crossed arms, down the sculpted surface of his washboard abs, past his towel-draped hips, down his long, lean hard-muscled legs. His right knee was bent, the toes of his right foot just barely touching the floor. She lifted her gaze back to his face. He was grinning at her, as usual, with that wild, wicked, come-and-get-me-baby look in his eyes, clearly enjoying her slow survey of his nearly naked body. But there was something else there, too, something dark lurking just behind the reckless bravado and sensual invitation in his gaze.

She glanced at the prescription bottles sitting on the kitchen counter. There were three of them, lined up in a row, each with a tiny tablet laid neatly out in front of it. "You haven't taken your pain meds yet, have you?"

His face went utterly blank for a moment. That was so not what he'd expected her to say. He recovered quickly, lifting one shoulder in a careless shrug. "Not yet," he said dismissively, both irritated by and uneasy with her question.

"Take them," she said.

Rebellion flared in his eyes.

"I'm a rancher," she said quickly, before he could give voice to all that masculine indignation and make some idiotic statement he couldn't back down from. "I've been around cowboys all my life. I've seen them get stomped on and gored and mangled. I've seen broken bones and cracked skulls and mashed fingers. I've even had a few myself. I know pain when I see it. And you're in pain. So don't be a macho idiot," she snapped, knowing instinctively that cooing feminine sympathy would only get his back up and make him feel he had to prove how stoic he could be. "Take the damn pills, Clay."

He stood stock-still for a second longer, holding her gaze, his mutinous and unruly, hers imperturbable and dispassionate. And then he gave a resigned sigh. "You're a mean, unfeeling bitch," he said conversationally and turned to pick up the pills.

"And you like that about me."

"Yeah. I guess I do." He tossed all three pills into his mouth at once, turned on the water in the kitchen sink and leaned down to drink directly from the faucet. "So—" he wiped his mouth with the back of his hand as he straightened "—now what?"

"Now we wait for those pills to take effect and then—" she stroked the chaps that were still lying across her lap "—I show you what I want you to do with these."

"What you want *me* to do with them?" He resumed his casual pose against the counter, his arms crossed over his chest in a way that best displayed his impressive physique. "Why do I get the feeling I'm not going to like what you have in mind?"

"Oh, I think you will," she said. "It's another one of my fantasies. And you've liked all of my fantasies so far, haven't you?"

He nodded. "So far."

"You'll like this one, too. I promise." She stroked the chaps again, with just her fingertips this time, the way she had stroked his skin the night before. "Trust me."

"Said the spider to the fly." He flashed her his wicked cowboy grin, the one deliberately designed to make women weak at the knees. "Maybe you should bring those into the bedroom so we can get started on whatever you've got in mind."

"We're not going into the bedroom. At least—" her smile was as wickedly seductive as his "—not yet, we aren't."

She was deliberately building up the anticipation, of course, and hoping to make him sweat a little while he wondered and worried about just what she had in mind, but she was also buying time for the pain pills to take full effect. She wanted him fully, completely focused on her when the time came, not distracted by pain. At least, that's what she told herself.

"You were terrific with the dudes today," she said.

"The dudes? You want to talk about the dudes? Now?"

"I just thought you should know. They were all very

impressed with you. Especially that little brunette from New York and her busty friend."

"The brunette's name is Arianna," he supplied. "The blonde is Stacie."

"Oh, you remember their names, do you?"

"Of course I remember their names," he said. "The two of them cornered me on the porch after supper and asked if I was interested in a three-way. Pret' near scared the piss outta me."

"Oh, dear." Jo Beth tsk-tsked with mock disappointment. "I may have to change my plans, unless… Does the idea of a three-way *really* scare you?"

"With those two man-eaters, it does. They're a couple of baby sharks. With really big teeth." He gave an exaggerated little shiver. "You have to promise to protect me from them."

"I promise to snatch them bald-headed if they get too close to you," she said, just a little more seriously than she should have if she'd really been teasing.

The spurt of jealousy—if that's what it was—disconcerted her enough to have her quickly changing the subject.

"If you want to know the truth, I was pretty impressed with you today, too," she said. "And I'm not talking about the way you fill out your jeans, although—" she smiled appreciatively "—you do that very nicely."

He tilted his head in acknowledgment. "I aim to please."

"And you do," she said. "On many levels. One of

them being the way you handled the dudes. No, let me finish," she said, when he would have interrupted. "I believe in giving credit where credit is due, and in admitting when I'm wrong. I pooh-poohed the idea and tried to make a joke out of it when Tom and Roxy suggested that you could be an asset on a dude ranch. But if you hadn't been there when the Bransons arrived, I'd have been stiff and unnatural, which would have made them uncomfortable, and everything would have started off on the wrong foot."

"You'd have pulled it together."

"Maybe. Eventually. But you being there meant I didn't have to. You're good with people. Real good."

He waggled his eyebrow. "I'm better in bed," he said, trying to turn the conversation to a subject that was more familiar and comfortable for him. He was used to being lauded for his physical prowess and his sexual expertise. He could respond to that kind of flattery with a knowing grin or a wiseass remark. Being commended for his social graces left him tongue-tied and embarrassed.

Jo Beth sighed. "I'm trying to show my appreciation here, and give you a compliment," she said. "The proper response is 'thank you.'"

"Thank you." He waited for two long beats. "Can we go to the bedroom now? You could show me your appreciation in there."

Jo Beth shook her head. "I'm going to have to make you suffer for that remark." She stood up, shook out the chaps, and held them out in front of her. A slyly considering look gleamed in her brown eyes. "I really like the way you look in these." She approached him with a slow, hip-rolling, hip-thrusting gait as she spoke, and held the chaps up to his waist, as if judging for fit. "They emphasize your tight little cowboy butt and showcase your package real nice," she said, and let them go.

He clutched at them automatically to keep them from falling to the floor.

"Put them on for me," she said.

"What?"

She slipped her fingers under the knot on the towel at his waist and pulled it off. "Put the chaps on."

"You mean, like this?" Clay was scandalized. "With nothing underneath?"

"Nothing but you," she purred.

"But that's… That's indecent."

"Why is it indecent?"

"Because it'd be like parading around in…in crotchless panties, that's why."

"And only women do that, right?"

"Yes." He immediately saw the trap he'd fallen into. "I mean… that is… Okay, yes," he said, deciding to stick by his guns. "Only women do that. It's biological."

"Biological?" She was really beginning to enjoy herself. He was blushing fiercely, a deep red flush staining his freshly shaved cheeks. "Really? Do tell me more."

"You know what I mean." He scowled at her, trying to look ferocious and in control despite the heat in his face. "Men are visual. We like to look. Women don't."

"Who told you that?"

"Nobody had to tell me that," he blustered. "It's a known scientific fact."

Jo Beth found him utterly adorable, completely appealing, and irresistibly sexy. He was so damned cute when he blushed.

"None of my women friends know it," she informed him. "We all like to look. We like to look at shoulders." She reached up and cupped her hands over the hard, rounded swell of his. "And biceps. We *love* looking at biceps." She smoothed her hands down over his arms. "And nice hairy chests." She drew her hands in, curving them over the bulge of his pectorals. "And washboard stomachs." Her fingertips trailed down over his belly. "And tight little cowboy butts." She moved in and reached behind him, cupping a cheek in each hand. "And cocks." She drew her hands forward, bringing them together, palms facing, fingers pointed downward, and lightly clasped his erect penis between them. "We love looking at cocks. Especially when they're big and hard."

"You can look all you want without me putting these on," he said stiffly.

Jo Beth sighed. "I guess I'll have to give you a little more incentive." She stepped back, far enough so that he could see all of her. Grasping the front plackets of her—*his*—shirt, she yanked it open. She shrugged her shoulders, letting it drop to the floor behind her, and spread her arms as if offering herself for inspection.

She was wearing one of the bachelorette party favors so thoughtfully supplied by LaWanda. The ensemble was made of slick wet-look black fabric. The bottom half was a tiny triangle that barely covered her pubis, and held on by narrow satin strings that tied in a little bow at each hip. The top half was a skimpy shelf bra that lifted and displayed her breasts without covering anything. She'd rouged her nipples and areolae with a slick red salve that made them look like glossy, ripe red cherries.

"Sweet Jesus God," he said.

She did a slow pirouette to give him the full view. There was nothing to see in back except a narrow black string that rode low on her hips and disappeared into the crease of her ass—and a temporary tattoo of a horseshoe on her left cheek.

"Sweet Jesus God," he said again.

"I thought you'd like it." She smiled wickedly, seductively, like Lilith and Eve and Jezebel all rolled into one. "Now it's your turn. Put the chaps on, Clay."

He hesitated.

"I knew you were a prude."

He put the chaps on.

"I feel like a fool," he said as he stood there in the galley of the trailer while she circled around him and looked her fill.

"Well, you don't look like a fool. You look magnificent." The chaps, clasped together below his navel with a silver belt buckle, rode low on his hips. The worn, supple leather covered his legs completely from hip bone to ankle, while leaving his entire groin area bare. Despite his embarrassment, he was beautifully erect. Jo Beth stroked the length of him with the tip of her finger, making his penis twitch. "If cowboys wore their chaps like this, rodeo would be the biggest spectator sport in the world," she said, and circled around behind him to enjoy the rear view. She patted his bare butt approvingly then leaned down and bit him. Not too hard, but not too gently, either. Just enough so he'd carry the imprint of her teeth for a while.

"What the hell was that for?"

"It's a brand," she said. "It means this ass—" she patted him again "—is mine."

He reached around and pulled her in front of him. "And what about this ass?" he said, cupping his hands over her cheeks.

"It's yours," she said. "For as long as you want it or until the end of the summer, depending."

"Depending on what?"

She shrugged uneasily, unsure how to answer him, unsure, even, of what exactly she'd meant by the careless statement. "On whichever lasts longest, I guess."

"I can't imagine not wanting it," he said. "Not wanting you. Not wanting this." He grasped her hips more tightly, urging her up, lifting her.

Jo Beth darted a quick glance downward. He had both feet firmly on the floor, his weight evenly distributed. She hopped up and wrapped her legs around his waist. The satin crotch of her G-string panties pressed against his throbbing erection. She locked her ankles at the small of his back and wrapped her arms around his neck, giving herself the leverage necessary to rub up and down against him, putting the pressure where she needed it most.

"I could come from this," she moaned. "Just this. Only this."

"Not yet," he said, and turned, setting her on the edge of the kitchen counter. He wrapped his fingers around her wrists, pulling her arms from around his neck, and pushed on her shoulders, pressing her torso back and away from him so that he could see her bare, rouged breasts.

Some of the red salve had rubbed off on his chest, but her nipples and areolae were still wet and glossy with it. They looked swollen and ripe enough to burst. He bent his head and drew one puckered nipple between his lips. The salve made his lips tingle.

"What is this stuff?"

"It's called Hot Cinnamon Kisses. It warms up the skin wherever you put it and makes it swell a little so that it's more sensitive."

"Is it safe?"

"LaWanda says it's made with all natural ingredients."

"Is it working?"

"Oh, yeah."

He bent his head again, drew her nipple into his mouth and bit down. Very gently.

She gasped.

He sucked the nipple into his mouth.

She shuddered and reached up to grasp his hair in both her hands, holding him there as if she would die if he moved away.

Still sucking on her nipple, he worked one hand between them, cupped her other breast in his palm and rolled her slick, swollen nipple between his fingers.

She came. Hard.

He sucked more strongly. Squeezed a little less gently.

She moaned and came again. Harder.

He lifted his head. His lips and tongue were tingling with sensation. "Can this stuff be used anywhere on the body?"

"LaWanda said it's mostly used for oral sex."

He plucked at her nipple, gathering as much excess salve as he could onto his fingers. "Take off your G-string," he said.

Jo Beth jerked at the bows on her hips and raised herself up a little, tugging the narrow strip of fabric out from between her legs. She was so aroused the friction of that alone was almost enough to send her over the edge again.

"Scoot forward to the edge of the counter and spread your legs as wide as you can," he ordered.

She obeyed.

He started to kneel down, found the angle awkward and the position uncomfortable for his bad leg, and stood up again. He wrapped an arm around her waist and pulled her to him, careful not to rub the salve off of his fingers. "Put your legs around me and hold on," he said. "It's time to go to bed."

He dropped her onto her back on the bed without bothering to pull off the bedspread, stuffed a pillow under her hips, and ordered her to spread her legs again.

She obeyed without hesitation.

Carefully separating the petaled folds of her labia, he exposed her clitoris. She was already slick and swollen, already fully receptive to his touch, already exquisitely responsive to the most fleeting caress. "Okay?"

She nodded.

He touched his salve-covered fingers to her most sensitive flesh, working it gently into and around the tiny bundle of nerve endings. She could feel the extra warmth immediately, and then the tingling began, little prickling sensations that were almost—*almost*—unbearable. Her head began to thrash on the pillow, and she tried to clamp her legs closed. He blocked her with his shoulders, holding her open and vulnerable, continuing the slow, steady strokes that were slowly, inevitably driving her crazy.

"Oh, God. I'm burning up. I'm on fire."

He pulled his hand away. "Does it hurt?"

"No. No. It burns. I burn. It—Oh, God, Clay. Don't stop. Please don't stop."

He scooted farther in between her widespread legs, bracing on his elbows, and used both hands to push back her labia and hold her open. And then he bent his head and sucked her clitoris between his lips. It was like an overripe berry against his flickering tongue, plump and juicy and ready to burst. He slipped his hands under her hips, cupping the cheeks of her squirming ass in his palms and concentrated all his considerable expertise and single-minded focus on bringing her to the most explosive orgasm of her life.

Jo Beth arched like an overstrung bow. The top of her head and the soles of her feet pressed down hard against the bed. Her hips pressed upward. Her body heaved. Her hips bucked wildly. Like the championship bull rider he was, Clay held on and rode it out to the end, refusing to turn her loose until she crested, high and hard and fast, screaming in exultation as she came. He waited until she started to come down the other side of ecstasy, and then sheathed himself in a condom and moved up her body and slid into her in one bold, hard thrust, ruthlessly driving her up again.

She reached down to hold on to him, her fingers curved, seeking purchase. They brushed the thigh straps of his chaps, the ones that snugged down tight just under his butt. She curled her fingers around them and held on, pulling him into her as she drove her hips upward to meet his pounding downward thrusts.

The straps of his chaps exerted an exquisite pressure against his scrotum. The residue of the cinnamon gel created a strange, tingling, tantalizing warmth in his penis. The tight clasp of her hot female passage soothed and excited and enflamed him. He let go and went under. Completion rolled through him in a wild, throbbing torrent of almost unbearable pleasure.

_11_

CLAY LIKED WAKING UP alone the next morning even less than he had liked it the morning before. And it wasn't just because he was horny again and wanted morning sex. He did, of course, but that wasn't the reason he was disgruntled and discontented and, well, just plain glum.

Actually, he wasn't quite sure _why_ he was feeling so melancholic. It didn't make any damn sense, especially after the fantastic night he'd had, and it wasn't like him.

He wasn't a moody kind of guy. He was easygoing and affable, most of the time. Happy with who he was and what he had, loving the free-and-easy life of the rodeo cowboy, perfectly content with living in a trailer and never having a permanent place to call home.

If it was sometimes lonely, if he sometimes felt restless and rootless and even a little bit aimless, well, hell, everything had a downside.

For the most part, he enjoyed the lifestyle, enjoyed the crowds and the accolades and perks that came with the silver trophy belt buckles. He liked the challenge of his chosen way of life, liked pitting himself against something bigger and meaner and more dangerous than he was and coming away on top most of the time. He damned sure liked winning and being the best at what he did. The prize money at the top wasn't bad, either; it made what he raked in from the sponsors just so much icing on the cake.

Sometimes he worried about losing his edge, about sustaining one too many injuries to compete anymore, about getting too old for the game, but that was another downside every professional athlete eventually had to face. But he wouldn't have to face it for years yet, he assured himself. And when the time came, he'd know, and he would bow out gracefully, while he was still on top.

He sure liked the women that came with the life he'd chosen—the free-and-easy buckle bunnies willing to tumble any available cowboy, the steady country girls looking for a little thrill to spice up their lives, the society debutantes looking to take a walk on the wild side. The women had always come easy to him, even before he'd started to win big and make a name for himself. He assumed they always would—at least, until he was too old to care anymore.

There was no downside to women that he could find. Not for him, anyway. Some cowboys he knew regularly got tied up in knots over some woman or other and made themselves, and everyone within earshot, miserable over the sorry state of their love life but he'd never been one to get wound up over any one woman in particular. There was always another one—just as fun-loving, just as pretty, just as passionate, just as accommodating—in the next honky-tonk, or in the next town, or sitting in the stands in the next rodeo arena. He'd never been one to want or need promises of any kind from any of them. Never been one to make them, either. And, yet…

It's yours. For as long as you want it or until the end of the summer, depending.

I can't imagine not wanting it. Not wanting you. Not wanting this.

They'd been talking about sex, of course, the way two people did when it was hot and exciting. It didn't mean anything. Not really. No promises had been made by either one of them, and none had been, or were, expected. It was just meaningless sweet nothings and sex talk meant to tease and arouse and feed the flame of desire. And, yet, somehow, as he lay there in his lonely bed in his lonely trailer in the lonely pearl-gray dawn, feeling unaccountably morose, he found himself wanting her words to be real, to constitute a promise, to mean something because, at some level, he'd actually meant the words he'd said.

He really *couldn't* imagine not wanting her.

Which, as far as he was concerned, was one big mother of a downside.

JO BETH WOKE in the gray predawn feeling ornery and out of sorts. Part of that was due, of course, to the lack of sleep the night before. She was always cranky when she didn't get enough sleep.

The other part of it—maybe the biggest part of it—

she attributed to the bitter resentment she felt at having to get up and get dressed and go back to her own bed after the most fabulous sexual experience of her life.

A woman should be allowed to wallow in a moment like that, to savor and enjoy it, to luxuriate in the afterglow. If the universe were just, she should be allowed to repeat the experience the next morning. At the very least, she should be allowed to wake up in the same bed with the man who had been instrumental in providing it.

Never mind that it had been her own decision to return to her own bed in the wee dark hours of the morning. Never mind that she had good reasons, sound reasons, for doing so. And never mind that she had been sorely tempted to just say to hell with all the reasons and greet the dawn in Clay's bed, in Clay's arms, tasting Clay's kisses—and let people make of it what they would.

It was nobody's business but hers if she'd taken up with another footloose-and-fancy-free cowboy; nobody's business but hers if she fell for him; nobody's business but hers if he stomped on her heart and left her pride in the dust when he moved on.

BY TWO O'CLOCK Jo Beth was crankier than ever and wishing she'd never heard of the dude ranching business. Unlike cattle, dudes couldn't be corralled, and they resisted being herded. Instead of staying within the boundaries she'd so carefully mapped out as dude territory prior to their arrival—the main house, the pool and play area, the meticulously staged and vigilantly supervised "dude-safe" network of corrals stocked with the most placid horses on the Diamond J, a couple of docile old cows and a few goats—they insisted on wandering all over the place and getting in everyone's way and, in general, making damned nuisances of themselves.

It wasn't as if she hadn't scheduled enough for them to do, either, because she'd taken all of the information on suggested activities supplied by the Dude Ranchers' Association and put it to good use. The first order of the day had been a sunrise trail ride with a chuck-wagon breakfast served at the end of it. After a hearty meal of flapjacks, bacon, sausage, eggs, grits, and cowboy coffee, all cooked over an open campfire, the dudes had the choice of attending a horsemanship clinic, going hiking or fossil hunting, or helping a couple of the cowhands move cattle from one pasture to another. If none of those activities beckoned, there was always the pool or the horseshoe pits or the Ping-Pong table or playing checkers on the porch or merely stretching out on the cushioned swing to read. And if all *that* wasn't enough to satisfy the urge for action, a guest could find golf or rafting available just a few miles down the road, if they were so inclined.

There was, Jo Beth thought morosely, no good reason any of them should be underfoot. And, yet, every damned time she turned around she seemed to be in danger of stepping on one of them.

"What are you doing? Huh? Is the cow sick? Can I watch?"

Jo Beth looked up over the withers of the Hereford cow she was doctoring and met the bright-eyed gaze of one of the Branson boys. He was peering at her over the top of the stall door. Only his eyes, his unruly mop of vibrant red hair, and the grubby tips of his fingers were visible over the railing. He was wearing a straw cowboy hat, obviously too big for him, pushed well back on his head to keep it from falling down over his eyes. Jo Beth tried not to glare at him. "How'd you get in here?" she asked.

"Through there." He pointed back behind him to the open barn door without turning his head. "What's that purple stuff you're puttin' on the cow? Does it hurt him?"

"Her." Jo Beth stifled a sigh. "And, no, it doesn't hurt. It's an antibacterial wash to keep the cuts from getting infected."

"How'd she get cut?"

"She got tangled up in a barbed wire fence."

"What's barred wire?"

"*Barbed* wire," she corrected him. "Not barred. It's a…" Jeez, how did you explain barbed wire to a city kid? "It's a special kind of fence made with twisted strands of wire with ah…" What was another word for barbs? "Really sharp points on it."

"How come you use it if it hurts the cows?"

"It doesn't hurt the cows if they stay away from it," she said, and wondered where her dude wrangler was.

He was *supposed* to be keeping the dudes out of her hair and out of trouble. He was obviously falling down on the job. Probably because he was too busy flirting with the two man-eaters from New York he'd been helping get ready for the trail ride today. Despite his protestations of the night before, he didn't appear to be the least bit scared of them *or* what they had in mind.

And why should he be? They were both exactly the type of woman stud cowboys like him usually went for— all flash and sparkle with curvy bodies, fluttering eye-lashes and glossy wet-lipped smiles. They were obviously out for a good time and were looking to Clay to supply that good time. And he, damn him, was look-ing back.

And why shouldn't he? she asked herself as she dabbed more antiseptic on the Hereford's wounds. He was a free agent, wasn't he? He hadn't made her any promises. And she didn't want any. If he wanted to bed down with a couple of bimbos from New York, it was no skin off her nose. She'd thought he'd had more taste, is all. But if he thought he'd bed down with *her* again after rolling around with those two, well, he had another think coming. Even though their "relationship" was fi-nite and destined to last only until he returned to the rodeo circuit, she expected it to be exclusive. Maybe she hadn't made her position clear to him.

Jo Beth Jensen didn't share her men.

At least, she amended, not when the sharing went on right under her nose. After all, she was certain both the Dallas cattle broker and good ol' Todd had other women in between their infrequent rendezvous with her, but they didn't carry on with those other women in front of her. Nor did she advertise the fact that she had other sex-ual partners in front of them. It was a matter of good manners and proper upbringing, is what it was. Both were something Clay Madison obviously lacked, because if he thought—

"Is the cow hurt bad?" the Branson kid asked.

"No." Jo Beth bit the word off through gritted teeth, then paused and took a deep breath, reminding herself of what she had at stake. The dudes were her new bread and butter, the key to her financial security. She had to be nice to them. "She *was* hurt bad," she said in a more moderate tone, "but it's not bad now. She'll be all healed up in a few days."

"Because of the purple stuff?"

"Yes. Because of the purple stuff."

"Can I help you p—"

"Don't open that door!" Jo Beth barked as he lifted the latch to the stall door.

The boy froze, his blue eyes widening in alarm.

Jo Beth clamped down on her impatience. "I'm sorry. I didn't mean to yell at you." *Where the hell was Clay?* "I just don't want you coming in here and getting hurt. Cows that've been injured can be unpredictable." Even cows that hadn't been injured were unpredictable, but it wasn't the time to go into that. "You could get kicked or stepped on."

"You're in there," the boy said, but he dropped the latch back into place.

"Yes, but I'm an experienced wrangler. I know what I'm doing. And, more importantly, the cow knows that I know what I'm doing, so she's comfortable around me. She doesn't know you and she might get nervous if you come in here." She flashed a conciliatory smile at the boy and hoped she didn't look demented. "And you don't want to make a cow nervous, especially in such a small space. They can kick the sh—stuffing out of you."

"What's a wrangler?"

Jo Beth bit back another sigh. The kid was making her dizzy with all his questions. "A wrangler is another word for cowboy."

"You're not a cowboy. You're a lady."

"I'm a woman. And a woman can be a cowboy."

"Nah-uh," he said. "A cowboy has to be a boy."

She lifted an eyebrow at him. "Says who?"

"It says so right in the word," he insisted. "Cow and boy. That means it has to be a boy. You could be a cow-girl, though," he added earnestly, in an obvious attempt to placate her. "It's almost as good as being a cowboy."

Jo Beth had to bite down on her tongue to keep from arguing *that* point with him. "Well, thank you very much," she said shortly and bent her head back to her task, hoping he'd take the hint and go away.

He didn't.

"What's the cow's name?"

"She doesn't have a name."

"She doesn't have a name?" His tone was faintly incredulous. "How come?"

"Because she's a cow, that's why. You don't name cows."

"Why not?"

"Because…ah…" How in the hell was she supposed to answer that? Tell him the truth? Tell him it wasn't smart to get on a first-name basis with an animal that was destined to become hamburger when her usefulness as a breeder was over? *And where the friggin' hell was Clay?* It was *his* job to answer the dudes' annoying questions. "There are nearly two thousand cows on the Diamond J," she said, finally. "If I gave this one a name, I'd have to give them all names. And I haven't got time for that. Besides, I'd likely run out of names before I ran out of cows."

"Do you have a horse?"

"I have lots of horses."

"Do they have names?"

"Some of them do. Some of them don't."

"How come only some of them ha—" The word ended in a surprised whoosh of air as a lasso dropped down over the boy's bright red head and circled his shoulders.

It had come silently, seemingly out of nowhere, a stiff "hoolihan" loop thrown with the wrist turned backward without a preliminary swing through the air. The technique was commonly used to avoid alerting or startling the animal being lassoed. It had floated over the boy's head without ruffling so much as a strand of his carroty-red hair or disturbing his hat.

He shrieked in excitement and immediately started to wriggle around like a roped calf, trying to get free of the lasso.

The Hereford rolled its eyes and tossed its head, shying away from the piercing, unfamiliar sound.

Jo Beth took a quick sideways step and put her free hand out, pushing against the animal's flank to let it know she was still there so she wouldn't get stepped on by 1,200 pounds of agitated beef.

"Hey, there, Spencer." Clay flicked the rope so that the loop slid down around the boy's torso to midchest. "Don't you know any better than to bother the jefe when she's working?"

"I'm not bothering her," the kid said, giggling as he squirmed to get free.

"Now that's where your plumb wrong, pard." Clay pulled the rope tight with another quick flick of his wrist, trapping the boy's arms at his sides. "She's doing delicate veterinary work there on that cow." He coiled the free end of the rope, slowly pulling Spencer backward, away from the stall door, as he did so. "She needs to give it all her attention and concentration to do the job right."

"But I'm not bothering her." The boy stopped squirming for a minute and turned around to look up at Clay with an earnest honest-to-God look on his freckled face. "I was just watching."

"Well, how 'bout you come on out to the corral and watch me an' T-Bone for a while? We're fixin' to have a ropin' class and show everyone how to throw a lasso."

The boy's eyes lit up. "Can I throw one? Will you show me how to throw one?"

"That's the idea, pard." Clay looked over the boy's head at Jo Beth and flashed her a grin, expecting to see an answering smile of approval for the way he'd stepped in and rescued her from the kid's unwanted attentions.

Jo Beth shot him a venomous glare in return.

He half turned, making a show of looking behind him to see whom she was trying to slay with her gimlet-eyed gaze. There was no one, of course. He glanced back at her and raised his brows questioningly, his grin still firmly in place. Surely she couldn't be glaring at *him?*

She jutted her chin at him, leaving no doubt it *was* him she was pissed at, then deliberately turned away and resumed dabbing antiseptic on the Hereford's wounds, despite the fact that the animal had already been well and thoroughly medicated.

Clay's grin faded and he took a half a step forward, bumping against the boy who stood between him and the stall. He reached down automatically, cupping the boy's shoulder to keep him from toppling over.

"Are we going to throw lassos now?" Spencer asked anxiously, obviously afraid the promised lesson was about to be canceled.

Clay hesitated for a second, his gaze questioning as it rested on Jo Beth's bent head. She refused to look up. Clay turned his attention back to the boy. "Yes, indeed," he said, "we are definitely going to throw lassos now."

Her head still down, Jo Beth flicked a furtive sideways glance at the pair to see how Clay was reacting to her snub.

He was grinning his cocky cowboy grin, as nonchalant as if he hadn't even noticed that she'd given him the cold shoulder. He reached out and playfully tapped the brim of the kid's straw cowboy hat so that it fell down over his eyes.

Spencer giggled with childish delight.

"Come on, pard." Clay grabbed the lasso where it snugged up against the boy's back and hoisted him off his feet. "It's time for your first roping lesson," he said, and walked out of the barn with his confident cowboy strut, his chaps flapping gently around his lean horseman's legs, his spurs jingling with every step, the giggling kid dangling from his fist like a sack of potatoes.

Jo Beth dropped her forehead against the cow's warm red hide. "Damn. Damn. Damn," she said, bouncing her head against the animal with each word. After a minute, she lifted her head and looked at the cow. "What in the hell is the matter with me?"

The cow didn't answer.

But Jo Beth knew without being told.

She was jealous and had been ever since 6:00 a.m. when she'd stood in the shadow of the barn door and watched Clay help those two buckle bunny wannabes from New York get saddled up for the trail ride.

"Oh, Clay," the one called Arianna had cooed, looking all big-eyed and helpless, her mascaraed eyelashes fluttering like agitated butterflies. "Could you help me here? My horse won't stand still so I can get on."

Clay had grinned his wicked cowboy grin at her, wrapped his big, calloused cowboy hands around the smooth expanse of bare skin exposed between the hem of her midriff-baring baby T-shirt and low-slung jeans, and hoisted her up into the saddle.

Jo Beth saw his grin widen when he came eyeball to navel, as it were, with the shiny gold ring adorning her exposed belly button. Arianna saw it, too. She arched her back to give him a better view, sticking her boobs out at the same time. The outline of the nipple ring on her left breast was clearly visible beneath the fabric of her bright pink T-shirt. Clay lifted his gaze to her face, taking in all the sights so blatantly displayed along the way, his eyes warm with masculine approval, his wicked hey-there-darlin' cowboy grin firmly in place.

"Could you give me a hand, too, Clay?" Stacie simpered. She was blond, busty and flagrantly feminine; everything, in fact, that Jo Beth wasn't. "My right stirrup is all tangled up somehow and I can't get my foot in it."

She leaned down in the saddle as Clay approached her, ostensibly to show him what the problem was, affording him an up-close-and-personal view of her very generous and grossly overexposed cleavage. He gave it the same lustful appraisal as he had her friend's pierced navel.

Jo Beth had stiffened—with disgust, she told herself—and turned away, stalking off into the interior of the barn with her teeth gritted tightly together and her hands fisted. She was standing the same way now, just outside the stall where the wounded Hereford resided, her hands clenched around the bottle of antiseptic and the soiled rag she'd used to apply it. Deliberately, she unclenched her fingers and set the bottle and rag on the storage shelf outside the stall door before she could give in to the temptation to heave them against the wall.

She still didn't know whom she was more frustrated with or what made her the angriest: those two simpering hussies with their obvious come-hither lures, Clay for being so easily lured, or herself for letting the three of them turn her into a quivering mass of insecurity and hurt feelings.

It wasn't supposed to be this way. She wasn't supposed to care what he did or with whom he did it. And she didn't, she assured herself, not really. It wasn't as if she had any *real* emotion invested in him. She and Clay were nothing but convenient sex partners. That was it. That was all.

It wasn't anything like the time when Tom Steele had come home from his final rodeo season with sexy, sassy feminine-to-her-painted-toenails Roxy in tow and broken their nonexistent engagement. She wasn't in love with Clay…. Well, she hadn't been in love in Tom, either, as it turned out, but that wasn't the point. The point was, she had *nothing* invested in Clay Madison except a few nights of hot sex. Not even her pride was at stake this time around because no one knew about their relationship—not that there *was* a relationship!—and, therefore, no one would feel sorry for her when it ended.

Seen in that light, it was obvious that what was bothering her was purely and simply rampant sexual jealousy. He was, after all, the best piece of ass she'd ever had. What woman *wouldn't* be upset at the thought of losing him to a pair of sexual adventurers from the big city?

The very thought of what she was being forced to give up made her want to scream. She kicked a bale of hay, instead, swearing under her breath at the injustice of it all. She was going to have to cut him loose and send him on his way. There was no other option. It wasn't only her unwillingness to share his sexual favors that was at issue; there was also the significant matter of the sorts of problems that could arise from a Diamond J cowhand indiscriminately boinking the guests. It was unprofessional on his part and, worse, it could conceivably lead to all sorts of unpleasant legal issues for the Diamond J.

She kicked the bale of hay again just because she was so damned mad, and visualized the toe of her boot making contact with the perky little butts of Arianna and Stacie. It was a very satisfying image, so she did it again. And again.

"You want to tell me what's got you so riled up?"

Jo Beth halted midkick and whirled around to see the primary object of her fury standing just inside the open barn door. Or rather, she saw his silhouette in the open door. Like that day at the water tank, the sun was at his back, outlining his broad shoulders and lean hips and casting his face in shadows beneath the flared brim of his black hat.

Her chin jutted out. "Aren't you supposed to be showing off for the dudes?" she said nastily.

Clay sighed. She was as mad as a wet cat, with her back arched and all her claws out. And he had absolutely no idea why. She'd been purring like a kitten when she left his bed last night and, as far as he knew, he hadn't done anything since then to warrant the sharp side of her tongue. Quite the contrary, in fact.

He'd had his nose to the grindstone all day, catering to the wants and the whims of the Diamond J dudes, and doing a damned fine job of it, too, even if he did say so himself. He'd even been enjoying it, which, when he took a minute to think about it, actually made perfect sense. He'd always liked playing to an appreciative audience and giving the fans a good show. Dude wrangling was just more of the same except on a smaller scale. He was still the star—and he didn't have to risk getting roughed up or stomped on to win the crowd's approval.

Well, not by a bull, anyway, he thought wryly, as he thumbed up the brim of his hat and locked eyes with Jo Beth. She looked ready to stomp the living shit out of something—and she was a damned sight meaner than any bull he'd ever faced in the rodeo arena.

"T-Bone is handling the roping lessons," he said, his voice and manner deliberately, almost condescendingly, calm.

It was, in his experience, the best way to push an angry female over the edge so she'd spit out what was bothering her. Nothing riled a woman more than a man who stayed patronizingly calm when she was itching for a fight.

"Shouldn't you be out there helping him?" she said. "That is your job, isn't it? To help with the dudes?" Her posture was tight with tension. Her voice snapped like a whip. "So why aren't you out there doing your job, cowboy?"

Clay propped a shoulder against the door frame. "As a matter of fact, it isn't," he said mildly. "My job, that is. I'm doing you a favor, remember?"

"Well, don't," she said fiercely. "I don't need any favors. I don't want them."

"What *do* you want, darlin'?" The smirk in his voice was designed to push her one step closer to the edge.

It worked.

"I'll tell you what I want." She stalked up to him, her eyes narrowed, her expression turbulent. "What I want is for you—" she jabbed him in the chest with her index finger "—to stop hitting on every passably good-looking female guest as if she were some hot-to-trot buckle bunny at a roadside honky-tonk. That's what I *want*—" she jabbed him again "—cowboy."

Clay was so flabbergasted he couldn't speak for a full five seconds. He honestly didn't know what she was talking about. She was the one and only woman he'd "hit on" since the run in with ol' Boomer, and that was only because she'd snapped him out of the sexual doldrums with her solo performance in the water tank.

"You didn't think I noticed, did you? Well, let me tell you—" she jabbed his chest again "—*everyone* has noticed."

He grabbed her finger, stopping her midjab. "Noticed *what,* for cryin' out loud?"

Jo Beth jerked away from him. "Oh, that's right," she jeered. "Pretend you don't know what I'm talking about. Pretend—"

"I don't have to pretend," he protested, beginning to feel the tiniest bit angry now himself. Being accused, tried and found guilty of something he wasn't even aware he'd done rubbed him the wrong way. "I don't have the slightest idea what the hell you're talking about."

"Oh, please! I saw you. I stood right here—" she pointed down to the brushed cement floor between their feet "—and watched the whole sorry show."

"Watched *what* show, damn it?"

"'Oh, Clay,'" she mimicked, "'my horse won't stand still. Oh, Clay, my stirrup is crooked.' And you!" she said scornfully. "Going along with the charade just so you could get your hands on those nitwit floozies and—"

Clay's nascent anger vanished. "You're jealous," he said, his sudden grin one of pure unalloyed delight.

"Don't flatter yourself," she scoffed, vehemently denying the fact that he'd nailed it in one. "Jealousy has nothing to do with it. I just don't want you leering at my guests. It's undignified and unprofes—".

"I don't leer."

"Yeah, well, you were giving a good imitation of it when that blonde stuck her boobs in your face."

"I'm a guy, for cryin' out loud. A woman sticks her chest in my face, I'm going to look. But that's all I did was look. I didn't *leer* at her."

"Ha!" she said eloquently. "You were leering so hard you were practically cross— What the hell do you think you're doing?" she demanded as he wrapped his hand around her biceps and began quick-stepping her away from the open barn door.

"Keeping you from making a spectacle of yourself."

"Keeping *me* from making a spectacle of myself? You're the one who was drooling all over the ménage à trois twins."

He yanked open the door to an empty stall and half dragged, half shoved her inside. Using his forward momentum and his hand on her arm as fulcrum, Jo Beth pivoted on her booted heel and headed back out the door. Clay pivoted with her, whirling around in a complete circle so that she ended up inside the stall again. He kicked the door shut and shoved her up against the wall, hard enough so there was a soft thud as her back made contact with the unpainted wooden planks.

Jo Beth snarled and pushed away from the wall, intent on escaping him.

Clay pushed her back and slapped his hands up against the planks on either side of her head, caging her where she stood. "Rein it in, Jo Beth," he said, his mouth next to her ear.

"You rein it in, cowboy." She shoved ineffectively at his chest. "And back off. I've told you before. I don't like to be crowded."

"I thought you were dead set on keeping your private life private."

"Yeah. So?"

"So pitching a jealous hissy fit in front of the dudes isn't the best way to do that." He jerked his head toward the open barn door. "You caught Miz Branson's attention when you started yelling at me."

"I didn't yell at you," she said furiously. "And I am not jealous."

Clay grinned at her. "You are, too," he said. "You're pea-green with jealousy." His grin widened. "I think it's real cute."

"And I think you're an egotistical, womanizing son of a—"

He stopped her words by leaning down and covering her lips with his.

She tried to twist her head away.

He followed the movement, bringing his hands to the sides of her face to hold her, keeping his lips sealed to hers until, finally, she stopped struggling and stood still, letting him have his way. But she didn't surrender. Her body was stiff. Her lips were sealed.

He deepened the kiss and gentled it at the same time, his lips parting over hers, his tongue teasing, his big hand cradling her face. He used all his skill to entice her to respond, giving her soft, moist, heated kisses that coaxed and cajoled.

She kept her lips stubbornly closed.

"Kiss me," he murmured urgently, feeling a sudden uncomfortable kinship with all the cowboys he'd known who got tied up in knots over women. "Kiss me, Jo Beth."

She kept her hands flat against the wall behind her, her fingers pressing into the wood, refusing to yield to the passion of his kisses and her own growing desire to return them.

He lifted his head slightly, just enough to look into her eyes. His expression was warm and melting, brimming with practiced persuasive charm. "Jo Beth," he breathed seductively, his breath warm against her lips.

She stared back at him, resolute and implacable. "You're still crowding me, cowboy."

Clay dropped his hands from her face and stepped

back. Obviously, seduction and charm wasn't going to work with her the way it had with every other woman in his life. He was going to have to rely on the truth.

"I didn't come on to either of those women," he said. "I'll admit I looked but—"

"You did more than look."

"Oh, hell! All right, yes, I did more than look. I flirted some, okay? But it was just a reflex action, like…" he searched for a metaphor "…like smiling at somebody who smiles at you. They flirted with me. I flirted back without even thinking about it. It didn't mean anything," he said earnestly. "It was just…" he shrugged uneasily. "It was nothing."

"That's not how it looked from where I was standing," she said. "From where I was standing, it looked like you were setting up the time and place for your little three-way."

"Well, so what if I was?" he said then, beginning to get just a little hot under the collar himself. He didn't like being accused of something he hadn't done. Of something he hadn't even *thought* of doing. "We're not exclusive. We haven't made any kind of commitment to each other. We're just having sex. So if I get the urge to do the horizontal tango with someone el—"

Something in her eyes brought him up short. They were still shooting sparks at him, but there was suddenly something under the anger. Not hurt, exactly, but something soft and vulnerable.

"Are we exclusive?" he asked incredulously.

"We're sleeping together, aren't we?" The expression

in her eyes might have softened but her tone was as autocratic as ever.

"And that makes us exclusive?"

"In my book, it does."

He eyed her consideringly. "That exclusivity work both ways?"

"Of course."

"Well, then, I'm sorry."

"Sorry?"

"For flirting with Arianna and Stacie. I didn't realize we were exclusive. Now that I do, it won't happen again." He smiled ruefully, with no hint of seduction in his expression. "Forgive me?" He reached out and touched her face, very lightly, brushing the backs of his fingers against her cheek. "Please?"

Jo Beth felt something inside her melt at his softly spoken entreaty, at the warmth and sincerity in his brown eyes, at the hint of desperation in his voice. There was something very attractive about a man who knew how to grovel. It made him even more attractive to her than he'd been before.

"All right," she said. "You're forgiven. On one condition."

"Which is?"

"Which is that you remember I don't like to share my toys," she said severely. "If it happens again you can just hitch up your trailer and hit the road, because I won't forgive you a second time."

12

IT DIDN'T HAPPEN AGAIN. When he left the barn that afternoon Clay resolved to treat the female guests with courtesy and consideration, but nothing more. They could flirt all they wanted but he wouldn't flirt back—even if it killed him. His smiles were warm and friendly, his manner was solicitous and helpful, and any flirtatious advances were met with the polite indifference of a man whose interests and attentions were elsewhere. It turned out to be ridiculously easy to do because, much to his amazement, his interests and attentions *were* elsewhere.

The two buckle-bunny wannabes from New York were puzzled at first by his sudden disinterest, then annoyed, and then, predictably, they cut their losses and focused their efforts on a more receptive audience.

"They're only booked through to the end of the week," Jo Beth said lazily as she and Clay lay side by side on their backs in his bed, cooling off after a sweaty bout of vigorous sex, "so they can't afford to waste time. They have to bag themselves a cowboy quick if they want to fit in a three-way rodeo before they head home."

"It's damned insulting to be so easily replaced," Clay

said with mock petulance. "Tends to deflate the male ego some."

Jo Beth rolled over onto her side to face him and reached out, curling her fingers around his flaccid penis. She rubbed the pad of her thumb, very slowly, around the plum-shaped head. Predictably, it began to harden and swell in her hand.

She grinned with feline satisfaction. "It doesn't look deflated to me," she said and rose up on her knees to straddle him. She took him inside her and rode him hard to a fast and furious climax for both of them. And when it was over, she slipped from the bed and started to dress.

"Stay," Clay said.

She shook her head. "You know I can't."

"Why?" The petulance in his voice wasn't faked this time. He was getting real tired of her getting up and putting on her clothes as soon as the sex was over.

"It's against the rules."

"You made the rules. You can break them." He propped himself up on an elbow and reached out, taking one of her hands in his. "Stay."

She was tempted. Oh, Lord, she was tempted. It would be lovely to cuddle in his arms and drift off to sleep. It would be heaven to wake up next to him, to be able to reach for him in the daylight. But it was a luxury she couldn't—*wouldn't*—allow herself.

She didn't dare.

Because she knew, come the end of the summer, if not sooner, he would leave. It was going to be hard enough to see him go as it was. It would be unbearable if he walked away from her with everyone watching. It would be just like the humiliating debacle with Tom Steele all over again, only it would be worse because she was older now and supposedly wiser and should know better than to get mixed up with a rodeo cowboy.

She could hear the whispers of her neighbors, those clacking tongues that would suddenly still when she walked into Bowie First Fellowship Church or the Come On Back Café or the feed store. She knew exactly what they would say, because she'd heard it before when Tom dumped her.

Poor Jo Beth, bless her heart, she hasn't got what it takes to hold on to a man like that.

The only way to save herself from all the pitying gossip was to make sure her friends and neighbors didn't have anything to gossip about. And the only way to do that was to make sure no one ever knew she'd fallen for another wandering cowboy.

"It's late." She disengaged her hand from his and resumed buttoning her shirt. "And I need to get some sleep." She smiled flirtatiously in an attempt to soften her refusal. "And you and I both know that won't happen if I stay here with you."

"What if I promise to be good?"

"Honey, you *are* good." Her smile warmed another few lascivious degrees. "That's the problem." She snagged her hat from the top of his dresser and put it on, pulling it down low over her forehead so it shaded her eyes. She touched two fingers to the brim, unconsciously copying his habitual salute. "See you in the morning, cowboy."

Clay lay there in the rumpled bed and fumed, feeling ill-used and unappreciated. It was a disquieting feeling, made all the more so because he didn't understand exactly why he was feeling that way. Or, maybe, he thought morosely, it was because he understood the reason all too well.

The sex, as always, had been great. Jo Beth was an uninhibited and inventive lover, who gave as good as she got. Unlike most women he'd been with, she didn't want or need any romantic trappings to enjoy sex. She liked it straight up and unadorned, with no strings and no promises and no commitments. And it wasn't just something she *said* she wanted, like a lot of women did because that's what they thought he wanted to hear. She meant it.

The problem was, he was a man who liked the romance of sex almost as much as he liked the act itself. He liked the stolen kisses and the accidental touches and the slap-and-tickle in a shadowed corner. He liked the butt patting and the pet names and the sly, teasing glances. All that was part of what made the mating dance so much fun.

But that wasn't really the problem. It wasn't what was causing the uneasy feeling in his gut and making him so uncharacteristically moody. What really fed his growing disquiet was the thought that maybe—just maybe—he wanted the other, more serious stuff that went with an intimate relationship. The strings. The promises. The commitments.

And that was as scary as hell.

It would mean huge changes in his life, bigger even than the changes that had come after ol' Boomer got finished tap-dancing on his carcass. A steady woman was a greater deterrent to a life on the rodeo circuit than any injury, especially if that woman was a wife.

He let the word rattle around in his mind. *Wife.* Was that really what he wanted from Jo Beth? Marriage? Settling down? Starting a family? Was that where his feelings were leading him? And if it was, was he ready for all the changes it would mean?

It seemed kind of crazy to think so. After all, it had only been a week since he spied her through the lenses of a pair of high-powered binoculars. Only six days since their first sexual encounter in Tom's barn. A man couldn't fall in love in a week, could he? No, that *was* crazy!

There had to be some other reason for the way he was feeling. Maybe all the pain medication he'd been taking since the wreck had finally fried his brain.

THEY HAD a cowboy competition and a campfire supper planned for the dudes' last full day. Jo Beth had sketched the broad outlines of the final festivities based on the literature supplied by the Dude Ranchers' Association, but Clay had been the one to take those sketchy plans and flesh them out so there was something for everyone. During the daylight hours there was a roping competition, a horseshoe tournament, a pie-eating contest and an exhibition of newly acquired horsemanship skills.

During preparations for the exhibition, Jo Beth came

up behind Clay while he was helping the oldest Branson boy saddle up. "It's José," she said, standing up on tiptoe to whisper in his ear.

"Hmm?" Clay muttered vaguely without looking up from the cinch he was tightening. He was still mulling over last night's startling revelations and hadn't come to any firm conclusions yet. It made him a tad incommunicative where she was concerned. "That should do it, Zac," he said and patted the boy's leg. "Remember to keep your back straight and your feet centered in the stirrups."

"José," Jo Beth repeated, as the boy trotted away on his horse to show what he'd learned over the past week. "He's your replacement."

That got Clay's full attention. He turned to look at her. "My what?"

"Your replacement." Jo Beth tilted her head toward the good-looking Hispanic cowboy who was helping Arianna Moore saddle her horse. "The third participant in the proposed ménage à trois."

Clay grinned. "Heaven help him," he said. "Those two will eat him alive."

Jo Beth grinned back at him. "Let's hope his shots are up to date."

After the stars came out there was a campfire supper followed by ghost stories, cowboy yarns, and a sing-along. T-Bone played a mean fiddle and one of the other Diamond J hands was proficient on the harmonica, so there was music, too.

"Tonight's the night," Jo Beth said when Clay

plopped down on the bench next to her after leading a line dance. "But, then, it would have to be, wouldn't it? Since it's the last night."

He plucked her mug of coffee out of her hand and took a sip. "The last night for what?" he asked, as he handed it back.

She gestured toward the cozy little group on the other side of the campfire with a tilt of her head. Three people—Arianna, José and Stacie—were sitting on a bale of hay meant to seat two. José was in the middle. "I think he's about to get lucky," Jo Beth said, as Arianna rose and took the good-looking cowboy by the hand. Stacie waited thirty seconds before she followed them.

"Better him than me," Clay said with an exaggerated shudder, and got up to demonstrate another set of steps to another country line dance.

Jo Beth remained where she was on the wooden bench, her back against the long wooden table, her hands curled around the heavy white ceramic mug, and watched him. His leg didn't seem to be bothering him tonight much at all—he'd gone easy on it during the day—and he moved gracefully across the bare wooden planks of the makeshift dance floor, making the complicated series of steps look easy. He was the star of the show out there among the dudes and other Diamond J cowhands, just like he was everywhere else. Dressed from head to toe in unrelieved black—black hat, black shirt, black jeans, black boots—he sparkled. He shined. He drew every eye in the place, male as well as female. People where drawn to his larger-than-life persona, his swaggering cowboy charisma, the innate physical appeal that went beyond sex to something even more basic and universal.

If they'd met in any normal sort of way, at a rodeo arena, say, he'd never have looked twice at her. He *hadn't* looked twice at her, not until he saw her buck naked and playing with herself in the water tank. In the normal everyday course of things a hardworking, wholesome, girl-next-door rancher like her wouldn't stand a chance with a sexy four-time PRCA champion bull rider.

Not that she wanted a chance, she reminded herself. Not really. She liked things just fine the way they were. It was all fun and games, and when it wasn't fun anymore, well, then it was over. That's the way she wanted it and that's the way it would be. No fuss. No muss. And no messy emotional attachments to come back and haunt her.

Jo Beth sighed and sipped her coffee and wondered how long it would be now before he'd go, and how she would manage when he did. Somehow, in only a week, he had become…well, not essential to her happiness— she'd only known him a week, after all—but important, nonetheless. He wouldn't break her heart when he left, she assured herself. Not that. Never that. But she would miss him. She'd miss his sly, roguish grin, and that wicked gleam in his hot-coffee eyes and his unbridled, uninhibited passion. She'd miss his easy way with the dudes, and his easy good humor and the sight of his tight cowboy butt encased in snug jeans as he went about his daily routine on the Diamond J. She sighed again at the thought of all she would be losing.

"He's definitely a man to sigh over." Carla Branson sat down in the space Clay had vacated. "You're very lucky to have him."

"I beg your pardon?"

Carla gestured at the dancers with her coffee mug. "Your cowboy. He's something else."

Jo Beth felt a flutter of panic in her stomach. "He's not my cowboy," she said.

"No? But I thought…"

"What did you think?"

"You struck me as a couple." Carla smiled. "A very nice couple."

"No." Jo Beth felt suddenly vulnerable and exposed, as if her innermost self was right there on her sleeve for everyone to see. She tried to tamp the feelings down, covering them up behind her usual icy facade. "No, we're not a couple," she said, very calmly, and took another sip of her coffee. "Clay works for me, same as all the other hands on the Diamond J."

"Oh. Well…" Carla Branson's gaze darted from Jo Beth's face to the dance floor and back again. "I could have sworn you two had something going." She grinned. "Something really hot. I mean, the way he looks at you—" She fanned herself playfully. "Yowza."

"There's absolutely nothing going on between us." Jo Beth pokered up like a spinster in a brothel. "I have a firm rule against getting involved with cowboys. They're unreliable."

"Oh. Well…" Carla said again. "My mistake."

Jo Beth sat silently for a few seconds, wondering if Carla Branson was the only one who had noticed she'd been making a fool of herself over another cowboy who was going to leave her as soon as he was able. She sincerely hoped it had only been Carla who'd noticed…whatever it was she'd noticed. Because it wouldn't be so bad if Carla were the only one. She'd be gone tomorrow at check-out time.

Jo Beth was more worried about whether the other hands on the Diamond J had noticed something, too. Had T-Bone noticed? Had José or Esperanza or either of the two teenagers from the Second Chance seen anything? Was the gossip even now being passed from neighbor to neighbor?

Poor little ol' Jo Beth has done it again, they'd say. *She's fallen for another cowboy.*

Heard this one up and left as soon as he was healed up, they'd say.

You'd think she'd know better, considering what happened with Tom Steele over at the Second Chance, they'd say. *You'd think, at her age, she'd know she doesn't have what it takes to hold on to a man like that.*

No one would stop to think that maybe Jo Beth had been the one to end it. No one would think that *she* had sent him on *his* way. She'd be the poor dumped almost-fiancé again, the woman who couldn't keep her man.

Jo Beth's ears started to burn as if people were already talking. Her insides went all cold and shivery with dread. Her face felt hot with embarrassment. She hated being talked about. Hated being pitied. Hated it! Hated it! Hated it!

"Are you all right?" Carla said.

"Yes, I'm fine."

"Are you sure? You look a little flushed all of a sudden."

"It's the fire," Jo Beth said, although they were sitting well away from it. "And the coffee. And I'm suddenly feeling kind of tired, too." She got to her feet and set her empty coffee mug on the table. "Will you excuse me, please? It's been a long day and I think it's finally caught up with me." She turned and left without waiting for an answer.

From his place in the line of dancers, Clay watched her hurry into the darkness beyond the edges of the campfire and disappear in the direction of the main house. He'd seen her talking to Carla Branson, seen her stiffen suddenly, seen the expression on her face go from easy and relaxed to something that wasn't either of those things. His first instinct was to go chasing after her and find out what was wrong, but he knew she wouldn't like that. It was against the "rules" she'd set out for their relationship.

If I hear a whisper of gossip, if I even think anyone suspects, it's over right then and there, and you're out of here.

Chasing after her would result in a whole boatload of gossip and speculation. So, he bided his time. He danced another line dance. He had another cup of coffee. He ate another one of Esperanza's honey-drenched *sopaipillas*. He patiently, competently shepherded the festivities through to their conclusion and waited until the campfire was doused and the dudes safely tucked away in their beds before he went after her.

HE COULD SEE THE GLOW of light around the edges of the curtains on her bedroom windows as he approached the back of the main house.

Good, he thought, *she's still awake.*

Not that that would have made any difference. If the windows had been dark, he'd have knocked anyway. First off, he was worried about her. And second…well, it was time to make a few things clear to Miz Jo Beth Jensen.

She answered the door at his first knock, yanking it open to glare at him furiously, and attacked without warning.

"You just had to make sure everybody knows about us, didn't you?" she hissed, keeping her voice low to avoid waking sleeping guests. "You just had to advertise your conquest and make sure everyone knows what a big cowboy stud you are."

Clay had meant to have a rational conversation with her, to lay his feelings on the line and tell her what he'd been thinking and inform her that he wanted to change the parameters of their relationship, but it was obvious she was in no mood to be rational. She was raring for a knock-down, drag-out fight, and Clay was just the man to give it to her.

He was the only man—the only *person*—on the Diamond J who could, because he was the only one who wasn't afraid of her icy temper.

He pushed the door inward, ignoring her efforts to keep him out by leaning on it, and stepped into the inner sanctum, the no-man's-land of the Diamond J. It was very like her, clean-lined, elegant, unadorned, without a frill or a ruffle in sight.

"Just what the hell are you accusing me of *this* time?" He bit the words off very precisely, his voice low and controlled and quiet in the stillness of her bedroom.

Jo Beth didn't heed the danger signals. She'd never seen him angry before, but then, few people had. She didn't know that the quieter he got, the angrier he was. And he was very quiet. Even if she'd known, though, she wouldn't have cared. Jo Beth was roiling over with conflicting emotions and needed to vent them. Only butting her head against something—or someone—was going to make her feel better.

"Carla Branson knows there's something going on between us," she said accusingly.

"Carla Branson is a very intuitive woman."

"Intuition has nothing to do with it. She *knows*."

"Are you saying I told her I'm banging the boss in my trailer every night?"

"No." Put like that it sounded ridiculous. "No, of course not. You wouldn't do that. Not in so many words, anyway."

"But?" He knew there was a *but* coming. He could see it seething in her eyes.

"But you don't need to *say* anything. You just need

to…well—" she waved her hand in front of his face "—you know."

"No, I don't know. I'm just a dumb cowboy, so you're going to have to spell it out for me in words of one syllable."

"You just had to look at me the way you do."

"Look at you? How do I look at you?"

"How the hell do I know how you look at me? You look at me, okay? And Carla Branson saw you looking and she *knew*. Everybody else probably knows, too. Or they've guessed. Either way, it doesn't matter, because it's over. It ends right here, right now, right this very minute."

He completely lost his cool. *"The hell it does!"* he roared.

"Keep your voice down, damn it." She hurried around him to close the door. "Do you want everyone in the house to know you're in my room?"

"I don't care if everyone in town knows I'm in your room."

"Well, I do!"

"Why? Why do you care so damned much about keeping us a secret? Are you ashamed of what we do together? Is that it? Are you ashamed to admit you have sex?" His voice got even lower, until it was little more than a vibration of sound in the air between them. "Or is it just that you're ashamed to admit you have sex with me?"

"No," she said vehemently. How could he even think such a thing? "No, of course not."

"Then why?"

"Because… Because…" How could she tell him the truth? How could she stand in front of him and admit that she was afraid of being dumped, that she was afraid of being gossiped about, that she was afraid of being pitied. It sounded so abject and needy, so hopelessly retro and helplessly, stereotypically feminine. It would just be too damned humiliating to admit the truth, to have him know that the hardheaded jefe of the Diamond J was really a spineless wuss who worried too much about what other people thought of her.

"I have control issues," she said finally.

"Control issues? That's your answer? That's all I get? You have *control* issues?"

"Yes." She jutted her chin at him. "I have control issues."

"Well, you're in luck, then, because I can help you with those."

"I don't need your— What the hell do you think you're doing?" she demanded as he reached out and pushed her backward onto the forest-green quilt on her bed with a quick, hard shove to the middle of her chest.

"I'm helping you with your control issues." He grabbed one of her boots by the heel, yanked it off, and tossed it on the floor behind him. "When I get through with you, you won't have any more control issues because, baby—" he yanked off her other boot "—you won't have any control left."

Jo Beth lay there for a second or two, stupefied by his statement, unable to believe he meant what it sounded like he meant. And then he leaned over her, reaching for the waistband of her jeans with both hands, galvanizing her out of her momentary inertia. She kicked out and flipped over, trying to propel herself off the other side of the bed. He curled his hand into the back of her jeans and yanked her back toward him. She felt the metal buttons on the fly of her jeans pop open under the pressure, and then she was flipped over onto her spine. She scrambled backward, scuttling toward the edge of the bed like a crab. He grabbed her ankle and pulled her flat. She doubled up her fists and started hammering at him. He ducked his head and hunched his shoulders, taking the hits she rained on him, and reached for the waistband of her jeans again. Curling his fingers under the denim fabric on either side of her hips, he yanked it down. She kicked furiously, but the action seemed only to help him peel the jeans—and her underpants—down her legs and off over her feet. He dropped them on the floor next to her boots. She began to fight in earnest, kicking and flailing as she tried to hold him off.

But Clay was bigger and stronger than her, and he was a professional rodeo cowboy. For nearly twelve years, he'd made his name and his living by sticking to the backs of wildly bucking bulls that weighed two thousand pounds and more, staying with them no matter how hard or how fast they twisted and turned beneath him. One skinny little woman, no matter how well toned—or how furious—was no match for him.

In minutes he had Jo Beth stripped down to her skin and on her back beneath him, held there by his weight straddling her thighs and his hands pinning her wrists to the bed.

She lay there, naked, flushed, breathing so hard she was panting, and glared up at him. "There's an ugly word for what you're doing," she snarled at him.

"Is there, now?" He smiled down into her face, his eyes gleaming with sensual intent, his lips turned up in that cocky, confident cowboy smile that put her back up and made her unbelievably hot at the same time. "Why don't you tell me what it is?" he challenged.

She opened her mouth to level the charge at him, but couldn't make herself form the word. What was happening between them wasn't rape or anything approaching rape. It was foreplay. And they both knew it.

"Oh, hell, just fuck me," she said.

"Oh, no." Clay shook his head. "Not this time. This time we do it my way."

Transferring both of her wrists to one hand, he curled the other under her waist and hoisted her up the length of the bed toward the headboard. It was an antique iron headboard, painted distressed white, with widely spaced vertical bars topped by cast-iron finials. There was a decorative maguey, a Mexican-style braided-grass rope coiled over one of the finials. Clay eyed it speculatively, but decided it wouldn't do for what he had in mind. The fibers were too rough.

Holding her carefully so that she couldn't twist away from him, he used his free hand to release the catch on his silver trophy buckle and slid the belt from the loops of his jeans. It was made of fine-grain leather, well-worn, soft and flexible. Using one hand and his teeth, he threaded the tongue through the buckle to form a small loop.

Jo Beth's eyes flared wide as she watched him, her expression hovering halfway between outrage and rampant sexual excitement. "You wouldn't dare," she said, knowing he would, *hoping* he would. No one had ever tied her to the bed before.

Without a word, he slipped the loop over her right wrist. Making sure it was snug enough so that she couldn't pull free, he threaded the end of the belt through the iron bars of the headboard and fastened it securely around her other wrist.

"Comfy?" he said, and patted her cheek.

She bared her teeth at him.

He grinned and levered himself up off her to stand by the side of the bed. "You start thrashing around, I'll tie your feet, too." His grin turned feral. "Spread-eagled."

"Bastard," she snarled, but she lay very still and watched him undress.

When he was naked, he sat down on the edge of the bed and looked at her. Just looked at her. She lay there with her arms raised above her head, her back arched, her small breasts upthrust with the hard pink nipples silently begging for his attention. One knee was slightly bent, her foot flat against the bed, her thigh turned coyly inward. Her slender body was lightly muscled and sweetly curved. Her skin was as pale as milk against the dark green quilt. Her long, thick braid lay curved across her neck.

It occurred to him that he'd never seen her hair loose,

never seen it cascading over her shoulders and down her back, didn't know if it was straight or curly or something in between. It was symbolic, somehow, of all he didn't know about her and all they had never shared.

He picked up the end of her braid, worked the elastic-coated band free, and speared his fingers through the plaited strands. Her hair was a heavily sun-streaked medium brown, thick and wavy, and incredibly soft between his fingers. Released from the confines of the braid, it was almost long enough to completely cover her breasts. He stroked his hands down the shining length, from the crown, down over her shoulders, to her breasts.

"Yes." She stretched luxuriously and arched her back, pressing her breasts into his palms. "Do me now."

However softly worded, it was a demand.

Clay lifted his hands from her breasts and placed them on the bed on either side of her. "Let's deal with those control issues, shall we?" he said.

Her smile was a seductive challenge. "Do your worst," she invited.

Clay knew she expected to be—*wanted* to be—ravaged, to be overpowered, to be taken with exquisitely controlled brute force. He knew she expected sexual gymnastics and sophisticated sensual games.

She was in for a surprise.

He smoothed her hair back gently, brushing it away from her face, and leaned down to press a soft kiss to the middle of her forehead.

She started as if he had poked her with something

sharp. "Clay," she murmured fretfully, expecting passion, uneasy with tenderness.

"Shhh," he said, and pressed another kiss between her brows. "I'm going to kiss every inch of your body. From here—" he touched his mouth to each eyelid in turn "—all the way down to your toes and back up again. And you're going to lie still and let me do it."

"Do I have a choice?"

"None at all," he said and bent his head to his self-appointed task. He kissed her cheeks and her chin and the curving line of her jaw. He kissed her throat and her shoulders, and the soft swell of her breast where it curved gently away from her rib cage beneath her armpit. He kissed her flat stomach and little jutting bump where her hip bone pressed against her skin and the soft, sensitive crease where her pelvis joined the top of her thigh. He kissed her knee and her shin and the top of her foot and the tip of her big toe. And then he worked his way up the other side of her body, giving her soft, sweet baby kisses that were almost more breath than substance, giving her tenderness, making love to her instead of just having sex.

Jo Beth was quivering by the time he started the return trip, her body drowning in sweet sensation, her mind drifting, floating on a warm sea of nascent emotion that threatened to overwhelm her with an unbearable longing for more. It terrified her. She stiffened against it, resisting the siren's call of tenderness, afraid she'd weaken and reveal just how much she needed it, and him.

"Untie me," she demanded. "I want to touch you. Untie me."

"Not yet," Clay said, and redoubled his efforts, trying to evoke a response from her that wasn't primarily sexual.

It was war, a primal battle of the sexes, except that the combatants had changed sides. He gave her everything he had, everything he was, offering her love and tenderness along with the delights of his body. She held herself back emotionally, and opened her thighs, offering only lust and physical passion.

Helpless to resist, Clay positioned himself between her wide-open legs and accepted the sensual invitation. He surged into her in one forceful thrust, both above and below, his tongue penetrating her mouth as his penis penetrated the slick, swollen walls of her vagina. She moaned and lifted her legs, clamping them tightly around his waist, crossing her ankles at the small of his back to keep him locked deep inside her and increase the power of his heavy driving thrusts. He slid his hands into her hair, cradling her head, cupping it gently in his wide calloused palms, holding her to him while he delicately ravaged her mouth. Their lower bodies slammed together with brutal passion, hard and fast and desperate, driving relentlessly toward completion. Their mouths melded in a paroxysm of reckless tenderness. She fought to maintain control, to keep a sense of self, to remain separate and apart from him no matter how closely they were entwined. He fought to absorb her into his very soul, to inhale her, to make her acknowledge him as more than a sexual convenience. Neither one of them succeeded completely, nor failed entirely.

They reached the finish within seconds of each other, shuddering together in a white-hot climax, pressing close until the trembling passed, both of them totally exhausted, physically replete and wholly dissatisfied despite the blinding strength of their mutual release. The aftermath was equally unsatisfying.

"Untie me, please," Jo Beth said when she could breathe again. Her voice was icy calm and utterly controlled, as if she were completely unaffected by the sensual storm that had just raged through them. It took every last ounce of strength she had to make it sound that way.

Clay unbuckled the belt that held her captive. "I hope I didn't hurt you," he said politely, chafing her wrists lightly as he released them. His touch was entirely impersonal, as if he hadn't just had his hands all over her naked body. It took every last ounce of willpower he possessed to keep from gathering her up in his arms again. The only thing that stopped him was the knowledge that she would resist him as fiercely now as she had when he first pushed her down on the bed.

He sat up on the edge of the bed and reached for the jeans on the floor. "I guess you're right about it being over," he said. "I'll hook up my trailer and leave in the morning."

13

Jo Beth spent the better part of the night alternately crying into her pillow, berating herself for being a stupid, spineless fool, and cursing Clay Madison to hell. None of the various activities had proved to be in any way productive. And none of them were in any way evident the next morning as she circulated in the front yard among her first batch of dudes, saying her farewells and helping T-Bone get their luggage to their respective automobiles.

Despite her personal unhappiness, she was gratified to see the satisfied smiles on the faces of her departing guests. It looked like everyone had had a good time. The man-eaters from New York had bagged their cowboy. The divorced dad and his teenaged son were still on speaking terms. The young couple celebrating their first anniversary were holding hands. And the four Bransons looked tanned and relaxed.

The first week of operation had been a success and it had proved two things to her: dude ranching was profitable and it was doable. Maybe a little less doable without Clay to help her, but she'd find someone else just as good with the dudes. Someone, moreover, whom there'd be no chance of her falling in love with, and no chance of her breaking her heart over.

Because, damn it, her heart *was* broken. It wasn't just her pride this time, the way it had been with Tom, although, God knew, her pride was going to take a hell of a beating. As soon as Clay's shiny black pickup rolled down her driveway and out onto the main highway with his trailer in tow, the whole county would be privy to the fact that she'd been dumped. By a cowboy. Again.

She calculated that about ten minutes after his truck was spotted heading out of town, some concerned friend and neighbor would drop by to commiserate with her and ask her what the hell she'd been thinking. Then, judging by what had happened when Tom had thrown her over for Roxy, it would take, oh, at least eight years before people stopped talking about it. If they ever did. She was a two-time loser now and, generally speaking, there wasn't any time limit on how long you could remain a topic of conversation when you'd made the same mistake twice.

"Where's Clay this morning?" asked Carla Branson. "My boys want to say goodbye to him personally."

"I'm sorry," Jo Beth said. "He's…busy."

"Not too busy to say goodbye to everyone," said Clay from behind her.

Jo Beth plastered a smile on her face and turned around to face him. "I thought you'd be packing," she said. Even to her own ears, the words sounded stilted and cold.

"Not all that much to pack," he said, his tone as icily

polite as hers. "Everything I own is already in the trailer."

"Hey, Clay! Clay!" The redheaded Branson boys ran up to him, clamoring excitedly for attention.

"Hey, there, fellas," Clay said. "What's up?"

"We're going home today," one of them said.

Jo Beth thought it was Spencer, but she wasn't sure.

"Yeah," said the other one, "and we wanted to give you this." He thrust his hand out, palm up.

His sibling plucked it out of his hand with two fingers and held it up to Clay. "We found it," he said. "It's a real Indian arrowhead."

"We wanted you to have it for teaching us to ride and lasso and stuff."

"Well, that's real nice of you both," Clay said, "but I can't take this. You found it. You should keep it as a memento of your vacation."

"Naw, that's okay. We're coming back next year. Mom said." He beamed up at his mother. "We'll find another one. Maybe you can even help us look?" the boy said hopefully. "We'd let you."

"That's a real nice offer, boys, but I won't be here next year."

"How come?" they chorused in unison.

"Why the hell—beggin' your pardon, ma'am." T-Bone nodded at Carla Branson. "Why the hell not?" he said to Clay.

Clay darted a quick look at Jo Beth. "I've been given my walking papers."

"You *fired* him?" T-Bone said incredulously. "What

the hell—beggin' your pardon, ma'am." He sketched another nod at Carla Branson. "What the hell for?" he demanded of Jo Beth.

"I'd rather not talk about this right now," Jo Beth said.

"But—"

"We'll discuss it later, T-Bone."

"But—"

"Later," she said, and turned away from him to continue with her farewells.

"What in blazin' hell did you do to make her mad enough to give you the boot?" she heard T-Bone whisper behind her, loud enough to be heard all the way down to the barn.

Clay's reply was more discreet but she heard it, too. "We had a difference of opinion," he said gruffly. "And since she's the boss, it's her opinion that counts."

She realized then, with those few words, said in just that disgruntled tone of voice, that he'd changed the entire complexion of the situation. Somehow, for some reason, he'd managed to create the impression that he wasn't leaving by his own choice. That he'd been sent packing. By her.

She could have made that very same assertion till the cows came home but, given her prior history, *she* wouldn't have been believed. Everyone would have just assumed that she was covering up her own foolishness and making excuses. But that very same assertion coming from Clay—and repeated by T-Bone, who was one of the biggest gossips in Bowie County—was golden and would be accepted as gospel without question.

She wasn't going to have to face the gossips, after all. And no one was going to "poor Jo Beth" her. Her precious pride was intact and unassailed—and it was, she realized, completely worthless to her.

"Well, shit," she said under her breath.

She knew, suddenly, what she had to do. She had to take a chance. She had to lay it on the line. She had to put herself out there and quit worrying about what everyone else would think of her. And if that meant looking like a fool, so be it. She'd look like a fool.

Without giving herself time to think about it, she stomped up the wide wooden steps to the front porch and grabbed the coil of braided rawhide rope hanging from the brass hook beside the front door. It was being used for decoration but it was a good stiff, strong rope made from bull hide, meant for roping steers by the heels. It should be plenty strong enough for what she had in mind. She uncoiled it, building herself a perfect "hoolihan" loop as she did so. With a quick, backward flick of her wrist, she sent it flying through the air.

It went right where she wanted it to—she'd been a junior roping champion in the under-twelve age group, after all—and whirled down over Clay Madison's head without touching his wide-brimmed black Resistol cowboy hat. She gave the rope another flick so that it settled down around his waist, and pulled it tight.

He stopped in his tracks but didn't turn around. He didn't so much as move a muscle.

Nobody did. Not Clay. Not T-Bone. Not any of the other Diamond J hands or any of the dudes who, moments ago, had been milling around the front yard like ants at a picnic. Everyone stopped and waited and watched.

The ball was in her court.

She took a deep breath and laid her pride on the line. "Stay," she said. "Please."

Clay didn't turn around. "Why?"

She took another deep breath. "Because I love you. Damn it to hell! I love you, Clay Madison."

There was a long tense moment of silence, and then Clay turned around to face her, a grin of pure happiness lighting up his face. It was his wickedly charming, cocksure cowboy grin, the one that turned her knees to water and sent fire racing through her blood.

"Come here, darlin'," he said, and yanked on the rope—hard—so that she came stumbling down the wide wooden steps and across the patch of lawn to fall into his waiting arms.

He clutched her to his chest, tightly, as if he would never let her go, and she held on just as tightly. She felt like crying and laughing at the same and did a little of both, sniveling happy tears into his shirtfront. And then he worked his hand between them, and lifted her stubborn chin on a curled forefinger.

"I love you, too," he said, and kissed her, long and hard and thoroughly, right there in the daylight, in front of God and everybody. She kissed him back—and to hell with what the neighbors might think.

Epilogue

IT WAS THEIR anniversary. Not of their wedding, but of
the day he had seen her through the lenses of Tom
Steele's binoculars.

Jo Beth sat, naked, in the water tank, just as she had
that day, her head resting against the concrete rim, her
eyes narrowed against the blazing Texas sun, her fingertips idly circling her swollen nipples as she watched
Clay undress in preparation for their annual private
party for two. The first few times they'd reenacted it,
he'd insisted on a faithful recreation of the original experience, right down to him watching her perform solo
from the vantage point of the tree-covered hillock yonder, before he joined her in the tank.

Now, after nearly five years of marriage, with a two-
year old back at the house under Esperanza's eagle-eyed
care, a second baby beginning to show itself in the slight
swell of Jo Beth's formerly flat belly, and a full com-
plement of vacationing dudes who couldn't always be
trusted to stay where they were supposed to, he was willing to deviate from a strict reenactment of the original
experience in favor of more efficient time management.

Instead of riding off to the tree-shaded hillock, he stood by the water tank, undressing as he watched her stoke and caress herself. His dark eyes were avid with lust, as if it were the first time he'd seen her do it. His breathing was fast. His pulse was visible in the vein at the side of his neck.

"Why don't you come on in and join me, cowboy?" Jo Beth invited when he was naked. "The water's great."

"You look like you're doin' just fine on your own, ma'am." His lips turned up in the wicked, roguish smile that still made her knees weak—or would have, if she'd been standing. "I think I'll just watch a bit longer, if you don't mind."

"But I do mind." She arched her back, thrusting her breasts more completely out of the water, and slid her hand down between her legs. "I need you. Bad."

"Well, in that case…" He started to step into the tank.

"Put your hat back on first," she said.

"What?"

"Your hat." She lifted her chin toward where his black cowboy hat hung on the saddle horn of his dappled gray mount. "Put it on."

"Why?"

"Because I have this persistent fantasy of you. In this tank with me. Soaking wet. Wearing nothing but your black cowboy hat." She continued to work one hand between her legs as she spoke. The other caressed her breasts. "It makes me hot just thinking about it."

He grabbed the hat off the saddle horn and put it on.

In too much of a hurry to wait any longer, she sat up straight, reaching for him as he stepped into the water.

One hand slid to the back of his thigh, pulling him down to her. The other curled around his rigid cock, as if to guide him to where she needed him to be.

"Hey there, now, darlin'." He took her hands in his as he sank to his knees in the sun-warmed water. "Let's slow this down some."

"But I want you inside me," she said almost petulantly.

"And you'll have me inside you." He turned her hands in his and pressed a warm kiss to the center of each palm. "Soon."

"Now," she demanded in her most autocratic tones.

"Soon," he countered again as he trailed his lips up her water-slicked forearm to the tender crook of her elbow. "I want to play first." He grazed her shoulder with his open mouth, careful to keep from bumping her with the rigid brim of his hat. "I want to touch you." He skimmed her collarbone with the tip of his tongue. "Kiss you." He nibbled at the curve of her neck. "Love on you for a good long while. And then—" he touched his lips to her ear, his breath hot with promise against her skin, his hat brim shading them both from the relentless sun "—when you think you can't take any more without going crazy, I'll flip you over and slip inside you and pound into you until the world explodes and you beg me to stop."

Jo Beth sighed languorously and let him have his way with her. It was a good way. The cowboy way.

Blaze™

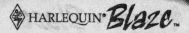

HARLEQUIN® *Blaze*™

The streets of New Orleans
are heating up with

BIG EASY
Bad Boys

Jeanie London

brings us an entire family of men with charm
and good looks to spare! You won't want
to miss Anthony DiLeo's story in

UNDER HIS SKIN
Harlequin Blaze #181
May 2005

Anthony is about to find out how an indecent proposal
fits into a simple business plan. When he approaches
Tess Hardaway with an idea to benefit both their companies,
she counters with an unexpected suggestion. A proposition
that involves the two of them getting to know each other
in the most intimate way!

Look for this book at your favorite retail outlet.

If you enjoyed what you just read,
then we've got an offer you can't resist!

Take 2 bestselling love stories FREE!

Plus get a FREE surprise gift!

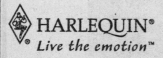

Blaze

HARLEQUIN® *Blaze*™

WEST SIDE CONFIDENTIAL
Secrets and seduction are off the record.

Popular Harlequin Blaze author

Joanne Rock

continues this series with

HIS WICKED WAYS
Harlequin Blaze #182
May 2005

He's on the run and not going back. But when Detective
Vanessa Torres struts into his life like a gun-toting cover girl,
Alec Messina thinks it wouldn't be so bad to share a few
confidences—especially if he can whisper them to her
across tangled sheets.

Look for these books at your favorite retail outlet.

www.eHarlequin.com

HBWSC0505